About the Author

Frank Dirscherl (b. 1973) is the author and editor of the Amazon bestselling *The Wraith* and *Beyond the Lens*. His series of *The Wraith Adventures* books have been enjoyed by multitudes of readers the world over. Other books in the series include *Valley of Evil, Crossfire, Cult of the Damned, Cry of the Werewolf* and *Sanderson of Metro* with more to come.

A professionally certified library technician, who has been working in libraries for over twenty five years, Frank has also worked at a medical practice in a data entry position, covered books for a book wholesale company, as a lecturer to children on the merits, and writing, of comic books, and as an online activist for social equality.

He lives on the south coast of New South Wales, Australia, with his beautiful wife Jennifer, where he is currently working on his latest piece of fiction.

For more information on Frank Dirscherl, please visit his website at **www.frankdirscherl.com**

Praise for *The Wraith*
Amazon bestseller

"I love the coloring job and specially the 'glowing' eyes on the chest of the character."

  – Guillermo del Toro, director, *Blade II, Hellboy I & II*

"I liked the story a lot... It's a very strong debut."

  Steve Englehart, writer, *Detective Comics, The Avengers, Green Lantern*

"I have read the novel (I couldn't put it down)... It is amazing to see how her (Leena) character evolves from Part I to Part II. At first she appears as every other 'girlfriend' in an action film, but those twelve months that pass obviously change her as a person and I love the person she becomes: tougher, but still human."

  – Amber Moelter, actress, *Catwoman: Copycat*

"I finished *The Wraith* book last night. I must say I enjoyed it quite a bit. The scenes kept playing in my head like a big budget Hollywood film. I mentioned earlier that I enjoy when the hero is put to the test physically and doesn't win the battle unscathed. Boy, (Frank) delivered that in spades!"

  – Jeff Welborn, artist, *Nightmare World, The Wraith*

"Genius + sweat + dedication = hard hittin' hero action! Go Aussie!"

  – Dan Lennard, writer, *People* magazine

"*The Wraith* is a wonderful throwback to the purple prose of the bloody pulps with a hero clearly descendant from the likes of the Shadow and the Spider. A fast, action-packed thrill-ride with great characters, both noble and villainous. Slam-bang kick off to a super new series. One I'm anxious to follow."

– Ron Fortier, writer, *The Spider, Brother Bones, Domino Lady*

"I became familiar with Frank Dirscherl's The Wraith from the comic book of the same name. When the first Wraith novel came out I just had to read it. I was not disappointed. The Wraith is a fast-paced thrill-ride. I'm looking forward to the upcoming sequel."

– Bobby Nash, writer, *Evil Ways, Fantastix, Lance Star*

"*The Wraith* (is) a really fun read. Have been a fan of Kenneth Robeson's Doc Savage and The Avenger books for years... *The Wraith* reminds me of Robeson at his best."

– G.R. Lawson, Publisher, General Jinjur Comics

"A short, pulp, superhero novel... Clearly more adventures to come with how this is set up."

– Richard Scott, *Super Reader* website

"*The Wraith* is an enlightening journey into the darkness of superhero fiction, and a worthy entry into both pulpdom and comicdom."

– Kevin Noel Olson, *Silver Bullet Comics* website

"*The Wraith* is a testament to Frank's dedication and talent. Other small press characters have come and gone, but The Wraith endures, because Frank understands what makes a classic character."

> – Richard Evans, writer, *The Canadian Legion*

"When it comes to superhero fiction and classic pulp stories, Frank Dirscherl channels those classic adventures of the past into *The Wraith* with ease and gives you a hero to believe in."

> – Stephen J. Semones, writer/director, *Beyond the Lens, Crossfire, The Wraith: Eyes of Judgment*

"Frank Dirscherl's writing is action-packed and reminds me why superhero fiction is so much fun in the first place!"

> – A.P. Fuchs, writer, *The Axiom-man Saga, The Way of the Fog, Undead World trilogy*

"Totally enjoyed this book. Good story, a real hero vs villain yarn. Can't wait to read the other adventures of The Wraith."

> – J. Newey, *Amazon*

Praise for *Valley of Evil*

"The second Wraith novel is an improvement, I think. Right from the start Dirscherl throws you into the middle of crazy action.... This book is a whole lot of superheroic pulp fun, and the good news is there seems to be more to come...I look forward to some more of the same."

> – Richard Scott, *Super Reader* website

"I think (Dirscherl) really captured a noir element with (his) voice."

> – Joshua Gamon, writer, *Abigail & Rox, Digital Webbing Presents*

"I did quite enjoy the books. Best of all, it wasn't overly sex-filled or gory—I can't stand most modern superhero comics that show such things or have the heroes just swear and swear. So *The Wraith* (and *Valley of Evil*) was just up my alley."

> – Greg Gick, writer, *The Werewolf of Rutherford Grange, Tales of the Shadowmen, Secret Agent X Vol. 2*

"The Dread Avenger is back. After battling the Cobra in his first prose adventure, The Wraith returns to face all new challenges from Metro City's greatest villains, most notably Hong Kong drug kingpin Ma Tzi. As with his first Wraith novel, Frank Dirscherl treats us to a pulp-inspired adventure that keeps readers on the edge of their seat. You have to read this novel in one sitting."

> – Bobby Nash, writer, *Evil Ways, Fantastix, Lance Star*

"In the past five years there has been a tremendous resurgence in pulp fiction centering on the old heroic pulps. Young writers have started taking up the mantle of old masters like Walter Gibson and Lester Dent and begun creating their own avengers in tales of genuine purple prose. Among the best of this new generation of wordsmiths is Australian, Frank Dirscherl and the exploits of his modern pulp paladin, The Wraith. This is grand pulp!"

   – Ron Fortier, writer, *The Spider, Brother Bones, Domino Lady*

Praise for *Crossfire*

"Stephen did a fantastic job of bringing Frank Dirscherl's character to life!"
- Adam DiTroia, composer, *The Wraith: Eyes of Judgment*, MTV, Fox Sports

"Loved the book!! Can't wait for the next installment..."
- Larry Mainland, actor, *The Walking Dead, Lawless, The Three Stooges*

"The action comes swift, and doesn't stop until the final pages. *Crossfire* tells a great story of betrayal and revenge."
- C.R. Blevins, writer, *A Western Tale*

"This was my first introduction to The Wraith and I was not disappointed. The action comes swift, and doesn't stop until the final pages.... If you love a good action/hero story, you will certainly enjoy reading *Crossfire*."
- Ally, *Amazon*

"Makes me want more...should be the next series on Netflix..."
- Bill Lancaster, *Amazon*

Praise for *Cult of the Damned*

"Only by the first three pages, Frank Dirscherl wonderfully captures a dark and mysterious atmosphere, one that leaves the reader with a cryptic and eerie sensation; one that makes me cold just thinking about it."

>   – Rennie Cowan, writer/director, *The Thriller Idol: A Tribute to the Legacy of Michael Jackson, Kade the Conqueror*

"Frank Dirscherl pulls you into the world of The Wraith from the first sentence and refuses to let you go until the last one."

>   – Stephen J. Semones, writer/director, *Beyond the Lens, Crossfire, The Wraith: Eyes of Judgment*

"The Wraith is one of my favorite characters and every time Frank Dirscherl puts pen to paper I know I'm in for a real treat."

>   – A.P. Fuchs, writer, *The Axiom-man Saga, The Way of the Fog, Undead World trilogy*

Praise for *Cry of the Werewolf*

"Frank Dirscherl delivers beyond measure... The solid characters, settings and story really propel you page to page and leave you hanging on for more."
- Stephen J. Semones, writer/director, *Beyond the Lens, Crossfire, The Wraith: Eyes of Judgment*

"Each new installment in *The Wraith Adventures* series is a guaranteed good time filled with high adventure, romance and pulpy fun. Dirscherl is at the top of his form."
- A.P. Fuchs, writer, *The Axiom-man Saga, The Way of the Fog, Undead World trilogy*

Praise for *Zombies Attack!* in *Metahumans vs the Undead*

"This compilation of superheroes vs evil offers top entertainment for superhero lovers! Frank Dirscherl and others are at their best with their contributed stories. I will now pursue other stories written by these authors, such as those involving Mr. Dirscherl's The Wraith. This type of reading enjoyment knows no end!"

    –   Ramona Wingart, writer, *Where is Brother Beaver?*, *Emily Suzanne Smith!*

Praise for *Werewolves Attack!* in *Metahumans vs Werewolves*

"Always a great read. Can never put it down once you get started... "

– Geraldine L. Lewis, Amazon

Praise for *Sanderson of Metro*

"Once shrouded in mystery, The Wraith's stunning origin is finally revealed. Dirscherl and Nash have written one hell of an adventure novel filled with myth, intrigue, and excitement. Highly recommended reading."

– A.P. Fuchs, writer, *The Axiom-man Saga, The Way of the Fog, Undead World trilogy*

BY FRANK DIRSCHERL

FICTION

The Wraith Adventures series

Sanderson of Metro (with Bobby Nash)
The Wraith
Valley of Evil
Crossfire (with Stephen J. Semones)
Cult of the Damned
Cry of the Werewolf
Vendetta - COMING SOON

SHORT STORY COLLECTIONS

Metahumans vs. the Undead
Metahumans vs. Werewolves
Metahumans vs. Robots
Metahumans vs. the Ultimate Evil
Lance Star - Sky Ranger Vol. 1

NON-FICTION

The Wraith: Eyes of Judgment - The Official Script Book & Movie Guide
(with Stephen J. Semones)
The Hitchers of Oz
Beyond the Lens (edited)

COMIC BOOKS

The Wraith #0
The Wraith: The Collected Editions #1-3
The Wraith: Books of Judgment Book One
Curse of the Cortes Stone (with Joe Martino & Scott Story)
Shadowflame: Bombed (with Joe Martino)

www.trinitycomics.com

THE WRAITH

SPECIAL EDITION

The Wraith Adventures #1

by

Frank Dirscherl

TRINITY COMICS

WOLLONGONG

TRINITY COMICS
PO Box 31
Wollongong NSW 2520

ISBN 978-0-646-98436-0

PUBLISHED BY TRINITY COMICS, February 2018
www.trinitycomics.com
FRONT COVER PENCILS/INKS/COLOURS by Splash!
COVER LAYOUT AND DESIGN AND INTERIOR DESIGN by Frank Dirscherl
EDITED by AP Fuchs
FIRST PUBLISHED IN 2003. REPUBLISHED TWICE IN 2005 & ONCE IN 2013
FIFTH EDITION

For more on *The Wraith: Special Edition*
visit www.trinitycomics.com

Text set in Garamond-Normal. Printed and bound in the USA

A catalogue record for this book is available from the National Library of Australia

NATIONAL LIBRARY OF AUSTRALIA

The Wraith Adventures series in correct reading order (including short stories)

- *Sanderson of Metro* *
- *Serpent Rising* * - COMING SOON
- *The Wraith*
- *Valley of Evil*
- *Crossfire*
- *Cult of the Damned*
- *The Things I Love the Most* in *Metahumans vs the Ultimate Evil*
- *Cry of the Werewolf*
- *Werewolves Attack!* in *Metahumans vs Werewolves*
- *Swamp Witch of Satan's Forest Part 1* in *Sanderson of Metro* (hardcover edition)
- *Sundown* in *The Wraith Dread Avenger of the Underworld* - COMING SOON
- *Sanderson of Metro* *
- *Serpent Rising* * - COMING SOON
- *Vendetta* - COMING SOON
- *Robots Attack!* in *Metahumans vs Robots*
- *Zombies Attack!* in *Metahumans vs the Undead*

So far...

The story goes on...

* The novels *Sanderson of Metro* and *Serpent Rising* take place partially in the past and partially in the present, hence their multiple listings above.

For Jennifer, as always; and to my family

THE WRAITH

~ Preface ~

Welcome to this Special Edition of my first novel, and the first in *The Wraith Adventures* series, *The Wraith*, celebrating the character's twentieth anniversary this year 2018. Now, some of you may be asking the question, if this novel was first published in 2003, then how can 2018 be the character's twentieth anniversary? Good question, but I have a good answer to go along with it. Bear with me here.

I created the character in 1998 as my answer to a growing frustration I had with the comic books of that time. Both the major publishers were starting to put out horrendous comics, where the gimmick ruled over substance, where splash pages were deemed more important than adhering to long well established canon, where rhetoric (the same rhetoric) was used constantly to describe almost every issue released that month. I well remembered the 1970s and 1980s where story was everything. Where continuity was honored and respected and where art was used to enhance the storytelling, not to take away and distract from it. So, I came up with The Wraith as my sort of character that could be used in stories that remembered and honored the stories of my youth.

Also around this time, I discovered the pulp novel, in particular that of The Spider, especially those written by Norvell Page (all were published under the author pseudonym Grant Stockbridge). I fell in love with those stories, for their action-packed adventures, their pacy narrative, their emotion-dripping melodrama. And, again, I thought to utilize that in my storytelling featuring my character creation The Wraith Dread Avenger of the Underworld ®

Now, while the character didn't see actual print in comic book form until 2002, and book form until 2003, he did exist online at a variety of message forums (remember the heady days of the online message forum, before Facebook, Twitter and the like took over?), both as an avatar and a character I wrote about from time to time. Mind you, he looked quite different back then, as his costume has evolved somewhat over the last twenty years, but his essence has always remained the same—that of an avenging hero that nevertheless has a rich and rewarding personal and social life. He isn't some moody, depressive like some similar characters out there.

So, here we are, twenty years later. It's been an amazing twenty years, not just for me, but for us all. The world has changed immeasurably. But, through it all, The Wraith has remained; steadfast, determined, ready to fight the good fight. May he ever remain thus.

As always, there are people to thank, and they're much the same as before, but they're always deserving of my gratitude. To my wife and family, you're the best. To my editor, AP

Fuchs, thanks for everything over the last eleven or twelve years or so. To my Trinity Comics team (you know who you are), thank you for always making me look good. And thank you, my dear readers, for taking my work into your hearts and homes. I do this for you, rest assured.

The following is not just a re-publication of the first novel in the series, but an *enhanced* version of it, featuring some corrections, some new additions (bringing the story more into line with its prequel, *Sanderson of Metro*) and a series of previews of two of the subsequent novels in the series, as well as an interview with yours truly and some special pieces of art and photos from the 2005 short film. I hope you enjoy this new Special Edition volume, and I thank you very much for your time and your patronage over the years. Believe me, I very much appreciate it.

Take care.

Frank Dirscherl
Wollongong, 2018

~ PART 1 ~

~ Chapter 1 ~

Metro City. A hothouse of evil and corruption. Since its birth in the late 1800s, much promise had been held for the city. It was meant as a metropolis to show New York and Chicago how to do it, planned as a beacon of light and hope. How ironic then, that since the prohibition era of the 1920s, Metro City had surpassed those other great cities as a den of iniquity and vice.

For a reason that was long since forgotten, crime lords had held the city in their sway, with city officials deep in their pockets. A few honest men and women endured, doing their best to stem the tide, but it was all they could do to simply tread water. As a result of the corruption, large portions of the city were neglected, in various states of disrepair, as city officials looked after their own interests and strove for their own protection. But there were still good people, those willing to fight for what was right and just.

Regular folk, who dreamed of what might have been, and worked, in their own small way, to achieve those dreams. People like the Commissioner of Police, George Harrison, and some of the officers under his command.

Then there was The Wraith...

For a few years now, a cloaked figure, calling itself The Wraith, waged his own personal war on crime. Very few truly believed in his existence. Only those whose word could not be trusted had seen this man, but he had made a difference. His legend spread, his myth had taken hold, and people began to hope once more for a better future. One of those men was police officer Michael Reeve.

* * * * * *

The Wraith staggered into the dark alley and came into the light of the full moon, his black cape no longer cloaking him in darkness, no longer shielding the Eyes of Judgment on his chest. Moving forward, he slumped against the wall to his left, panting and heaving. For what seemed an eternity, he rested there. Then, gathering his strength, continued forward.

Coming to the end of the alleyway, The Wraith looked up into the night sky. The corpulent moon was almost blinding in its brightness. He reached for the ladder to the fire escape, and pulled. With a tired groan, the ladder lowered to the ground. He gasped, discomfort enveloping him, and began his ascent. He worked his way slowly upwards.

At the top, The Wraith tried to climb over the balcony's railing but stumbled and fell onto several potted plants that were on the rooftop and lay there. He gathered his strength once more. In the weak balcony light, his injuries became clear. Blood oozed from a deep wound to his chest, the blood having splattered onto his arms where he had tried to stop its flow. His right shoulder was wounded just as badly.

Weakly rising, The Wraith eyed the sliding door leading into the apartment. One step forward. Another. And another. One more, and he was there. He banged furiously on the door, panting, barely able to stand on his own strength, and waited for a response.

"What the...?" came a voice from within. A light turned on in the apartment, but nothing clear was visible through the curtains.

* * * * * *

The curtains ripped open and the man The Wraith had come to see appeared. Michael Reeve stared silently through the door's glass.

"Oh my lord," he said, though The Wraith could only see the words mouthed from behind the door's glass.

Without further hesitation, Michael unlocked the door and slid it open. The Wraith took one careful step inside, and collapsed to the floor.

Michael was stunned beyond belief. Here was his idol, the man whom nobody, at least nobody he knew, believed in save himself. He had been denigrated for his beliefs and honesty by many of those he worked with for believing in what was no more than a ghost story. But now, here was The Wraith, in his own apartment.

"You're the...the..." was all he could utter.

The Wraith slowly rose to his knees, and Michael saw the horrific wound on his chest.

"You're wounded. You need help," he said.

"Must pass it on before...before it's too late," The Wraith said.

Michael helped him to his feet.

"I'll help you to the sofa, then I'm calling for an ambulance," he said.

"No. There is little time left," The Wraith said. "You are the one, Michael Reeve."

"You...you know my name?" Michael stammered.

"You're the one..." He slumped against Michael's chest then raised his hands to Michael's temples. A burst of light and then...

Darkness.

~ Chapter 2 ~

Earlier that day, Michael Reeve was preoccupied. Never a morning person, he walked to his car parked in his apartment's underground garage assuming this day would be as any other. A tall man in his late twenties, with thin brown hair, his heart was heavy, his mind filled with the turmoil of his job. Being a Metro City Police Officer could do that to you.

Soon out in city traffic, Michael's car phone buzzed.

"Hello," he answered.

"Michael, it's Bob Sloan. Listen, I think you should maybe take today off."

"Why?"

"That anonymous survey we took a few weeks back, remember?" Bob sounded weary. "You put your name to it, and, well, some of the guys are having a field day with some of what you wrote...about The Wraith."

"What? How did that get out? I thought the results would be kept confidential and *anonymous*? Anonymous survey, remember?" His teeth ground together.

"Station tom-toms. You know how it is."

He waited a moment. "I'm not going to let a few morons stop me from doing my job, Bob."

"Hey, I just thought I should warn you. You're due some time off anyway. But if you do come in, just be careful."

Michael pulled into the Metro City Police Department parking lot, still determined not to let anyone stop him from giving his best at a job he loved so much. Crooked cops had been trying to sway him for as long as he'd been on the force. When that failed, they resorted to taunts and cruel jokes. Now it appeared on the cusp of escalating.

He got out of his car, hoping that anyone feeling like pulling a joke on him would at least leave his car alone. He went into the building and straight to the locker room, past several of his co-workers. He heard the snickers, saw the grins, but said nothing. Reaching his own locker, he shoved his bag inside, trying his best to ignore those around him. Three of his colleagues came toward him, surrounding him. The tallest of them, Stanley Crane, spoke first. "Hey Reeve, better wait 'til we're all gone before changing, or we might see your Wraith costume underneath." He laughed, joined by the other two.

Michael ignored them and began changing into his police uniform.

"Nope, nothing there. Must be in his locker then," said the man to Crane's left. He reached for the locker door, but Michael quickly slammed it shut.

"Hey!" the second man cried.

Michael turned and faced the three of them. Crane, as was his wont, grinned at him with what was clearly an attempt at charm. He failed. "Come on, Reeve. We're just having a little fun here."

"Yeah right," Michael replied. "Are you going to stand there and watch me undress?"

Before any of them could answer, a raspy voice cried out, "Reeve! You in here?" It was Captain Bellows, the local area commander. Crane and his stooges scattered, the few others in the locker room went back to whatever they were doing. Captain Bellows rounded the corner.

"Ah, there you are. Bill said you were coming in today."

"Why wouldn't I?"

Bellows, a gruff, silver-haired man in his fifties, stood before him, concerned.

"Michael, you've got a ton of leave accumulated. Why don't you—"

Michael cut him off. "Not you too? Why is everyone so eager to stop me from doing my job?"

"Don't take that tone with me, Reeve. We're understaffed as it is, worse than ever. Believe me, I'd rather have you here than not." Bellow's tone then took on a more conciliatory note. "Look, you're a good cop, and God knows we need more of those. But the heat's on you right now, kid, so maybe it's best for you to take some leave and let things blow over for a bit."

"Is that an order, Sir?" he asked.

"No, it's a suggestion. A strong suggestion though. Think about it."

Captain Bellows turned and left.

Frustrated and confused, Michael finally thought it best to leave, to clear his head if for no other reason. Back in his car,

Michael drove through the city, not really knowing where to go or what to do. He could go and visit his girlfriend, Leena Patterson, but he decided against that. Not in his current frame of mind. He didn't want her to worry, and really wasn't up to talking about it at any rate. Aimlessly driving wasn't in his plan either. The only thing he could think of was to hit the gym, where he could vent his frustration in some semblance of a productive fashion.

Pulling into a parking spot in the lot behind the police gym, Michael heard a muffled explosion. Getting out quickly, he looked at the front right tire.

"Oh, great. Just what I need," he said.

Annoyed, he opened the trunk. The spare was gone. *Dammit,* he thought. He forgot that last week he was forced to use it on one of the rear tires and hadn't yet gotten a new one. Cursing himself for not taking care of things, he yanked his gym bag from the trunk, pulled his cell phone from his pocket, and slammed the trunk lid down.

"Leena, hi. I'm at the gym. I need a ride home tonight. Why? Because one of my tires burst and I forgot to replace the spare." Michael tried to keep calm for Leena's sake but after the jerks at work this morning and now this, he didn't know long he could hold out. "5:30? That'll be fine. See you then, Honey." He felt a little better. Hearing Leena's voice always brought a smile to his face; a warmth to his heart. He entered the gym.

Michael hit the machines with vigor, working each one as if he had something personal against them. He wasn't a regular gym-goer, not overly muscular, but he was fit and had a reasonably good stamina. After finishing with some weights, he headed for the treadmill, and ran until he thought his heart would burst and a stitch claimed his side. Stopping to catch his breath, he began to wonder if his honesty was really worth all the trouble at work. Maybe it was best to just stay quiet and do the job and leave it at that? See no evil, speak no evil. But that wasn't his way. Neither was giving up. He briefly thought to continue with his run but saw the time on his watch, and knew Leena would be here soon to pick him up.

In the locker room, he had just started to reach for his bag when Stanley Crane walked in to join him. Michael hadn't known Crane was also a member of this gym, but now he almost regretted being a member himself.

"So, this is where you got to. I'm surprised you're not out looking for your superhero pal." Crane sat beside him. "Face it, Reeve, you just don't belong on the force. You just don't fit in."

Michael felt like replying, but his blood was still boiling too close to the surface and any further trouble wasn't what he needed right now. He pulled his bag from his locker and locked it.

"You afraid, Reeve? You scared of me? You should be. You never know what could happen one day." Crane gave him that "charming" grin again.

"Don't threaten me, Stan. I've got better things to do than listen to your rubbish." He got up to leave.

"Hey, listen—" Crane said.

"Bye, Stan." Michael left.

The sun shone bright as he exited the gym. Walking amongst the bustling city foot traffic, his heart lightened when he saw Leena's car already waiting for him at the curb. He hopped in.

"Hi honey," Leena said cheerfully. Her strawberry blond shoulder-length hair looked lovely, the afternoon sun glinting slightly in her oval-shaped glasses. He just smiled at her weakly. "You look tired. Rough day?"

"You could say that. Or you could say it was one of the worst days I've ever had."

Leena looked concerned. "Well, you're done early. Are they still giving you trouble? Maybe you should—" She stopped when he looked at her. He'd heard her entreaties to leave the force before. He was as disinterested now as he ever was, despite the difficulties he was going through.

"You deserve so much better, Michael," she said. "You could do anything you want."

"I *am* doing what I want. I want to make a difference. I want to try and make things better in this city." His head hurt with frustration.

Leena, too, had heard this before. Michael knew deep down she supported his decision, whatever it would be, though she would continue to try to encourage him whenever she could.

"What happened today?" she asked.

"Remember that questionnaire I told you about?" Leena nodded. "Well, somehow the results leaked out and, of course, most of the cops in my station are focusing on what *I* said. I shouldn't have put my name to the damn thing even though it was supposed to be anonymous. I should have known better." Michael pinched the bridge of his nose.

Leena adjusted her glasses. "You were being honest. I don't want you feeling as though that's some kind of character flaw. It's not! Your honesty is what makes you a good cop. And a good man."

She smiled at him and he couldn't help but feel better. He took her right hand in his, smiled back, then kissed it. No words were spoken. None needed to be.

Leena started the car and slowly edged out into the busy Metro City rush hour traffic.

~ Chapter 3 ~

The full moon had risen about an hour before a classic Daimler sedan came to a halt in an alley in the dingy warehouse district of Metro City. A slight breeze swept through between the buildings, bringing with it pieces of trash and filth.

Inside the car, the driver, Max Horton, a stocky Irishman with a shock of red hair, lit a match. The light also brought into view the rear passenger—The Wraith. Max lit his cigarette.

"Wait here," The Wraith said, his voice raspy and deep.

"Sure thing, Chief," Max said. "You sure you don't need me to stand point?"

The Wraith silently exited the car. "I shouldn't be long, if that tip-off proves to be accurate. Stand by."

Max turned, but The Wraith had vanished, merging into the sinister darkness of the Metro City night.

* * * * * *

Atop a warehouse alongside the waterfront, an armed guard paced steadily. At the building's edge, he peered over, looked down onto the street and the adjacent bay. The ocean lapped at the dock, its sound almost hypnotic. The guard turned and walked to the other side, scanning the rooftop. The breeze had lessened now, though it was still chilly. The guard stood at the edge and stared out at the bay, as if transfixed by the echo of the tide hitting the shore.

Behind him, The Wraith dropped silently on the rooftop, having leapt from the building opposite. The Wraith crept toward the guard, the man completely unaware of his presence. There was a slight tap on his shoulder. He turned and was met by a powerful left, which ended the confrontation before it had a chance to start.

The Wraith removed a small coil of rope from his belt and restrained the guard, lest the fellow regain consciousness before the job was done. He looked around and spotted his goal–the rooftop entrance to the warehouse. He opened the sunroof and slithered inside.

Inside the warehouse, there was a bustle of activity. Armed guards moved about. As The Wraith watched on from his heightened vantage point, he thought the amount of firepower on display here confirmed his intel as correct.

Workers secured and hauled large crates to a central point on the warehouse floor where several vans waited, ready to be filled with the no-doubt-important cargo. Overseeing the operation was a well-dressed, portly man—Robert Latham, legitimate businessman, the wealthiest man in the city and head of the largest crime cartel on the eastern seaboard. He inspected the work going on around him then turned to the bald, burly man walking alongside him.

"Is everything set?" Latham asked.

"Everything's just about packed and ready to go," the man replied.

Latham tousled his hair and smiled. "Then ship 'em out. Those Afghans want these weapons yesterday, and I don't want to disappoint them. Not after what happened with their last shipment."

"Sure thing, Mr. Latham."

High above the warehouse floor, atop the intricate maze of catwalks, The Wraith continued to listen. Yes, Latham was readying a huge shipment of arms to Asia, Afghanistan being the apparent prime port-of-call. He grinned through gritted teeth at the accuracy of the information he had been able to obtain from his source. He had no intention of allowing this shipment to leave Metro City.

Latham continued walking, inspecting the progress of his men. At the end of the aisle, he stopped, turned and nodded his approval. Before he could resume his supervision, The Wraith dropped like an ethereal phantom into the heart of the largest group of workmen, and stood just ahead of Latham himself. The men scattered. In an instant, the battle started. The Wraith's fists and feet moved with speed, connecting with the jaws and stomachs of the men advancing toward him.

A group of workers from the other end of the warehouse quickly appeared, rounding a large pile of crates, machine guns in hand. The Wraith rolled to one side, dodging the barrage of bullets that came, and settled behind a large section of highly stacked crates. He quickly peered around, counting Latham's men. A quick view of at least six greeted him, before he was forced to duck back, just managing to avoid another volley of firepower.

"Damn you! I won't let you stop this shipment!" Latham screamed.

The Wraith stalked silently along the line of crates, trying to gain a better view to further assess the situation.

"I'll make you a deal, Wraith," Latham shouted. Footfalls clamored on the cement, Latham's remaining men surrounding him. "You come out here now, and I'll make your death quick and painless!"

At the other end of the long line of crates, The Wraith peered around its corner. Seeing Latham being protected by his men, he pulled back.

"There's no escape, Wraith. Why not just come out and accept your destiny, as I have mine?" The Wraith didn't move. "I'll give you two minutes to come out here and join us. I promise you, you won't like the alternative!" The Wraith reached down to his belt, producing four small, marble-shaped pellets from a pouched compartment, and jiggled them in his hands. Readying himself, he reached around and tossed the pellets toward Latham and his men. The pellets rolled along the ground, quickly arriving at their intended target. Several of the men looked down. Latham, a short man, unable to see over his men, couldn't make out what they were looking at.

"What? What is it?" he said.

A biting hiss and smoke erupted from the pellets, engulfing Latham and his group. The men were soon coughing and wheezing, nothing but smoke around them.

"What the—" Latham said. "Stay close!"

The Wraith saw his opportunity and took it. Running, he launched himself into the smoky cloud. From within, sounds of intense battle almost shook the warehouse. Fists and feet flew, but it was over quickly. In just on a minute, as the smoke slowly began to dissipate, The Wraith was taking care of the last of the men.

The smoke thinned and The Wraith advanced toward Latham.

"No, stay back," Latham said, hand outstretched.

The Wraith stopped his advance, stood silently for the briefest of moments, then spoke. "I have come for you, Robert Latham. Justice must be served."

"Justice? You talk to me of justice? Whose justice? Yours? You know what you can do with *your* justice?"

The Wraith said nothing. The Eyes of Judgment on his chest gained an uncanny shimmer, yellow and inhuman. Latham was sweating.

"Now, finally, you will feel the pain you have caused, the anguish you have inflicted" —The Wraith grabbed Latham by the throat, forced the crime lord's face into his chest, and forced him to feel the effects of the Judgment Stare. Anyone who gazed into the Eyes of Judgment could not help but feel the pain and inner torment of every victim of their crimes; their deceit, their evil. One who has gone through this must do their utmost to atone for what they have done. To do anything less would drive them insane, or worse— "and the guilt you deserve!"

Latham gave in to the Eyes of Judgment, helpless to do otherwise. Mystical energy of ancient origin crackled from the Eyes. Latham struggled in The Wraith's iron grip, but it was hopeless. His expression was first of anger, arrogance, violent denial. Then it slowly started to change. Pain began to show, but not physical pain. Stuck fast, Latham couldn't hold on. He screamed in terror, the years of his wrong-doing evidently finally bearing fruit on his psyche.

With tears in his eyes, Latham suddenly stopped. He chuckled, and regained his composure as no-one ever inflicted with the Judgment Stare had before. The Wraith, bewildered, released his grip on the crime lord. He hadn't expected this.

"Did...did you think it would be that easy?" Latham said. "Did you think you could take me like some dime store hood?" Latham lashed out with a right—a weak one—but managed to connect with The Wraith's chin. The Wraith staggered back a little, more from surprise than from the power of the blow. "Oh sure, you had me there for a moment. I could feel things I have no wish to ever feel again. But I like to think I'm strong willed enough to overcome your little mind games. I haven't come all this way, worked this hard, to let you run over me with a little guilt trip. I've accepted what I've done—who I am—long ago."

Latham retreated a safe distance and yelled, "Carl!"

A deafening shot rang out—and The Wraith gasped. He looked down at his chest. Blood oozed from a gaping wound. The bullet had pierced his heart. The Dread Avenger slumped to the floor with a thud. While he writhed in agony, Latham casually approached him.

"I had this whole night planned. I can't tell you the trouble you've caused me over the years, time-and-time again. I was finally forced to take charge myself. You've continually proven to be untouchable to anyone I've ever sent after you. And my plans led us here." Latham swaggered with sickening confidence. Now by The Wraith's side, he crouched down, and put his hand on the hero's shoulder. "It had to end like this. A battle of two titans. It was either you or I." He smiled. "I'm glad it was you."

His injuries nearly overtaking him, The Wraith lashed out with a punch. It connected, albeit weakly, but it was enough to throw Latham off his guard. In an instant, The Wraith was on his feet in an incredible show of will and determination, and ran for the large paneled window at the far end of the warehouse. With a desperate leap, he jumped through the window. Landing hard on the pavement outside, shards of glass scattered around him, The Wraith scrambled to his feet, reached up to his injured right shoulder and cradled it.

He ran into the night, the darkness enveloping him.

* * * * * *

Latham and Carl were at the window, straining to see where The Wraith had gone off to. Carl moved to follow, but was held back.

"Let him go," said Latham. "He won't last. Not the way he was bleeding. I can't believe he still had the strength to get up, let alone run out of here."

"What do we do, then?" Carl asked.

"Nothing. I think our Wraith troubles may finally be over," Latham said. He turned and walked back further into the warehouse, whistling a small tune. Carl stayed by the window for a moment, checking in all directions, but saw nothing.

* * * * * *

Back in the alley, still seated in the driver's seat of the Daimler, Max Horton lit another cigarette. Not normally a regular smoker, Max couldn't help it today. For some reason he was nervous, worried. He furrowed his weather-beaten brow and tried to shrug off the feeling. Puffing away, he looked about him, trying to remain alert, but the alley appeared deserted. Thinking to check behind the car, he turned his head and saw The Wraith sitting in the back seat.

The cigarette dropped from his mouth. He scrambled to get it back between his teeth before he burned himself. "Geez! You nearly gave me a—"

"Drive," said The Wraith firmly.

He saw The Wraith's terrible wounds. "You're wounded. We need to get you—"

"It's too late for that." He wheezed heavily. "Drive! It's time. I can feel it, feel the energy building for release." The Wraith stopped for another breath. "You know where to go. You...you know the plan."

~ Chapter 4 ~

Michael's inner city apartment building was decent, though nothing grand. The building was in fairly good condition despite being advanced in age, but it looked well lived in. Michael's apartment was small, with two bedrooms, able to house two people in theory, but in practice was another matter. Michael kept it clean and tidy, but it was marked by the complete absence of personal photos. No signs of family could be seen anywhere.

It was late, but Michael and Leena were still awake. The two were kissing on the beige-colored sofa. After a few moments, they broke, Leena smiling, her hazel eyes carrying that special something that stole Michael's heart when he first saw her. He smiled back and brushed her hair from her smooth face.

"I have to go," she whispered.

He pulled her close. "Stay."

Leena sighed. "You know I have that early morning meeting. Sue's in another of her tizzies and all the staff have to be there to hear her latest scheme." Leena leaned back and smiled cheekily. "If I stay, I definitely won't be sleeping."

She stood and headed for the small kitchen behind them.

Michael rubbed his neck. "Okay, okay, I understand. You know, we still haven't finished that talk about you moving in here."

Leena re-appeared, a bottle of water in hand. "Yes, we have." She took a sip. "We decided that your place is too small for the two of us. Heck, *my* place is too small for us."

Leena sat beside him. "Michael, we've been down this road before. Until we both have enough money, until we're both ready for such a big change..."

He took a deep breath. "You're right, you're right...but..."

"Didn't we agree to take this one day at a time?"

"Okay," he said, resigning once again to ending this discussion in her favor.

Leena glanced at her watch. She quickly picked up her glasses and handbag, and gave him a peck on the cheek. "I love you, but I really have to go. I'll see you tomorrow?"

"Sure."

At the front door, she turned and blew him a soft kiss. "See you tomorrow, honey." And she left.

Michael leaned back, grumbled. Since when did his life get so complicated? He rubbed his neck once more before reaching forward for the afternoon newspaper on the coffee table. Reading the headlines, he saw the announcement of a record profit for Latham Industries. He snorted in disgust. Everyone on the force knew Latham wasn't just the honest businessman, the "kind" philanthropist, he presented to the public.

Heck, Michael thought, *most of the force is probably in Latham's pockets as it is.*

He was exhausted, more tired than he'd felt in a long time. His life was going nowhere fast. His dream job was hardly a dream come true anymore. His apartment was too small for anything useful, and he was too poor to afford better. His girlfriend, whom he loved more than anything, seemed to love him back, but she was also hesitant to commit, apparently happy with the status quo and nothing more.

The frustrations of his daily existence were beginning to take their toll. It was late and he was too tired to head to bed just yet. His eyes began to sag, as though lead weights were dragging them down.

Darkness was beginning to creep in, when a loud banging at his balcony door shocked him awake.

"What the...?" He got up and strode over, then ripped the curtains open. What he saw sent shivers up-and-down his body. It was The Wraith.

"Oh my lord..." was all he could utter.

Quickly, not thinking this could be a hoax, he unlocked the balcony door and slid it open. The mythical hero stumbled inside.

"You're the...the..." He couldn't finish.

The Wraith began to rise, and Michael finally recognized the blood on the hero's chest. "You're wounded. You need help."

The Wraith, with Michael's assistance, was helped to his feet. "Must pass it on before...before it's too late." The Wraith's voice didn't sound as deep and intimidating as Michael thought it would. Perhaps now it was a mere shadow of its former glory. The Wraith was wheezing, beginning to bring up blood with every staggered breath.

Michael began to help carry The Wraith over to his sofa. "I'll help you to the sofa, then I'm calling an ambulance."

The Wraith stopped him. "No. There is little time left. You are the one, Michael Reeve."

Michael couldn't believe The Wraith knew who he was. "You...you know my name?"

"You're the one..." The Wraith fell against his chest and raised his hands, grasping Michael's temples.

Before Michael could respond, a bright flash of light exploded around them, then everything went black.

* * * * * *

Michael's eyes opened slowly and awkwardly, almost as if they had been glued shut. He sat up in bed, and glanced around him. The bedroom was almost as large as his entire apartment, and handsomely furnished. Michael was stripped to his waist, revealing a much more muscular, toned physique than was possible without extensive training. Extensive training *he* had never undertaken.

He tried to stand, but was wobbly on his feet. His head hurt and his vision was blurred. The bright morning sun streaming in from the large windows didn't help the matter any.

"Who am I?" he found himself whispering. He furrowed his brow; his mind was fuzzy.

When he tried to make his way to the door, it began to open. A tall, slim, elderly gentleman with silver hair and friendly eyes, clearly the butler of the house, entered, carrying a breakfast tray. The wonderful aroma helped alleviate the pain in Michael's head ever so slightly.

"Good morning, Sir," said the butler, unfurling the morning newspaper.

"Morning..."

The butler began pouring the coffee. "I trust your nightly forays were successful again, Sir?"

Michael looked at him with bewilderment and was unable to answer.

~ Chapter 5 ~

Inside Michael's apartment, at least a half dozen police officers and a few detectives moved quickly about. Some took notes, some dusted for prints, some were discussing the situation at hand. In the center of the living room a large blood stain shone bright on the carpet. A crime lab officer knelt beside it, scraping samples, putting them inside a tubed container.

Detective Bob Sloan, a burly man in his fifties with pug-nosed features, stood alongside the stain.

"What have we got, Tom?" he asked the crime lab officer.

Tom stood, his samples now stored.

"Apart from this blood stain, nothing," he said. "So far, no prints; the place has been wiped clean as best I can tell. No weapon, no real evidence of anything violent having taken place here. If not for all this blood..."

"Any theories, then?" Sloan asked.

"Well—"

* * * * * *

It was morning. Leena stood at Michael's door. She wasn't sure what to make of cops and men in suits in Michael's apartment and was almost infuriated by them being there.

"What is this?" she asked sharply.

She pushed her way through the crime scene tape blocking her way. A man rushed toward her, trying to keep her back.

"What are you all doing here?" she asked, starting to worry.

"This is a crime scene, Miss—?" the man probed.

"Patterson," she said. She was beginning to get frantic, a feeling which grew enormously upon sight of the large blood stain on the floor. "Where's Michael, what's going on here?" If anything happened to him...

She barged past him, not really knowing what to do, but she knew she couldn't just stand still. He turned to face her.

"I'm Detective Bob Sloan. I'm heading up this investigation." He stuck out his hand for a handshake, and though she recognized the name, she didn't take it. "Some neighbors called the police after finding the door to Mr. Reeve's apartment open early this morning, and finding blood on the carpet. We don't know yet, but with Mr. Reeve's absence, the blood might be his. With Mr. Reeve's whereabouts unaccounted for..." said Sloan.

She couldn't bear hearing this. "His name is Michael, and he's one of *you*! You're acting like..." Tears began to trickle down her face. She'd never been as scared as she was this moment.

Sloan, seeing this, tried to act more human. "Miss Patterson, believe me, we're doing all we can at this early stage. I promise you, we'll find out exactly what happened here. We're not going to let one of our own down like this. Michael was a friend." He placed a hand on her shoulder. "I know he's been going through a lot at work lately. Trust me, not all of us were a part of that. The entire force isn't on the take, let me assure you of that."

Leena smiled weakly, but she was having trouble controlling her emotions. She had to, though, or she'd never find out anything more. She turned to face the man standing alongside Sloan, clearly a C.S.I. officer by the equipment he was carrying. "Tell me something. What happened here?"

He looked grim. It worried her.

"It's too early to tell, really, but...but it doesn't look good," he said.

Shock began to overwhelm her. Sloan came over to her and, judging by the look on his face, was trying to make up for his gruff attitude earlier.

"Miss Patterson, I'm sorry," he said. "You shouldn't have had to see this. Please, go home, and let us do our jobs and we'll get back to you as soon as we can. We'll need your statement at some point as well, but we'll leave that for now." He started to usher her out of the apartment but she was reluctant to go. "Please."

"I...okay. Just...just please find out what happened to Michael." She slowly made her way past the tape and exited.

* * * * * *

Tom stood shoulder-to-shoulder with Sloan. "What do you make of that?"

"I don't know. Could just be a concerned girlfriend, could be something more. I got her to drop her guard slightly by my change in attitude. I think I'll take a different approach next time I see her."

Tom looked at him, and indicated he knew what that meant. Heaven help her if she were involved in this somehow.

~ Chapter 6 ~

The sun shone brilliantly on the large, inner city Sanderson House mansion. This was old time money and how. Built only a few years after the city's inauguration, it was a testament to "Old Man Sanderson," who built the monolith, a display of his standing and power in the community. Though dead, his stature kept the house standing even as the city rose and stretched around it.

Now, the house was the home to his descendant, Paul Sanderson, the reclusive multimillionaire, who returned to the family property almost four years ago after years abroad. Since then, he had rarely been seen, gaining notoriety almost as vivid and lurid as that of Howard Hughes or JD Salinger. And, although the public had no idea, Sanderson was also the Dread Avenger of the Underworld—The Wraith.

Inside the house, in the main bedroom, long-time Sanderson butler Jonathan Simpson had just served breakfast, though not to Paul Sanderson. Michael stood there, dazed somewhat. What was strange, however, was that Simpson was acting as though nothing were wrong, as though Michael *were* actually Paul Sanderson.

"My...forays?" Michael asked, still confused.

"Yes, Sir. I assume the job at hand, whatever it may have been, proved successful?" the butler said, his English accent thick and pure.

Michael shook his head then strangely seemed to finally understand what the butler was talking about. He remembered who he was, or, *who* he thought he was. "Successful enough, Simpson." Incredibly, Michael *believed* himself to be Paul Sanderson.

"Very good, Sir. I shall return to my other duties, then."

Simpson left, making as dignified an exit as he did an entrance. As soon as he left the room, and as Michael sat to breakfast, Max Horton barged in, looking tired yet determined.

"You don't look the worse for wear," Max said.

"No major damage, Max. Small cut here on my shoulder" —Michael pointed to his right shoulder— "and a killer headache. Tell me, though, were last night's actions successful? I'm a little hazy this morning on the details."

Max appeared a little nervous, but held his demeanor. "Erm...you remember. You broke up a major drug ring. Foiled some robberies, too."

Michael was puzzled, but nodded in faint agreement. "Yes, yes of course." He stood, having barely touched his food, and faced Max. "I'm not up to scratch this morning. I'm just going to fester and squirm in the house if I don't go downstairs and try and iron out the kinks."

"Sure thing, Chief. Just don't overdo things. You had a pretty busy night last night," said Max, following him along the upstairs corridor.

Now downstairs, the two entered the library–probably the most impressive room in the house—and a favorite of Sanderson's. The walls were lined floor-to-ceiling with books, the shelves and furnishings a deep, classical mahogany. A large writing desk was on the left, also timbered in a rich tone, while a leather wing chair was on the right, the perfect location for a quiet and cozy night's reading before a large, open fireplace.

Max removed a small remote control device from his pocket, similar in size and shape to that which operated the average television set, and pressed a small button at its center. With a slight hum, a portion of the bookshelf before them pushed forward then slid to the left, revealing a dark passageway. Michael casually walked inside, Max behind him, and reached along the adjacent wall, flicking the light switch on.

A large, cavernous room opened up before them under the sharp light overhead. The Wraith's Lair; a secret hideaway within the house that served as The Wraith's headquarters and refuge. The two stepped onto a small, round floor pad—an elevator—which at the flick of another switch, slid downward toward the central section of this expansive quarters. Now on ground level, past banks of computers, a laboratory, and a wall lined with Wraith costumes, they reached the fully equipped gymnasium at the far end of the Lair.

Michael turned to face Max. "A good workout should clear my head."

Max eyed him with concern. "Are you sure you're all right, Chief?"

"Just this headache. It'll soon pass."

Max sighed, obviously reluctant to press the issue further. "I'll be about my business, then." He turned and left, and was up the elevator in an instant, the secret door above closing with a soft thud behind him.

Michael looked blankly at the wall of Wraith costumes ahead of him. He couldn't help but shake the weird feeling that he'd never been here before.

Thinking himself crazy, he flipped the hair from his forehead and remembered he didn't have hair this long. He marched over to the Lair's bathroom and stared into the mirror. Amazingly, his hair had either grown quite a lot overnight, or he didn't get it cut last week as he thought he had. His head hurt even more at the thought of this. Sighing, not being able to make sense of anything, he pulled open a drawer under the sink and removed a pair of scissors. Soon he emerged from the bathroom with a much shorter, more dignified style befitting that of Paul Sanderson.

Returning to the gym, he looked around him, trying to decide on which piece of equipment to tackle first.

* * * * * *

The Metro City Police Headquarters building was, unfortunately, one of the major casualties of the city's losing battle with finances. Once a fine specimen of Gothic architecture, the structure had long since fallen into disrepair due to years of budgetary cutbacks. The majority of the available money was being funneled into the pockets of crooked officials and a backward political system. The front light was shattered, bricks were cracked, paint was peeling. Hardly an example to be proud of.

Inside, Detective Sloan and his partner, Detective Rosa Perez, a pretty, but tough looking Latina woman who wore little to no makeup, were talking with Leena. Or, at least, they told her it would be a talk, to simply get her statement for their investigation into the disappearance of Michael Reeve. Interrogation was more like it.

"You saw Michael last night, is that correct? What time did you leave?" Sloan asked.

"Did you have any disagreements? A fight?" Perez asked.

Leena looked at them through glassy eyes. "Am I a suspect?"

Perez leaned in close. "We're just covering all the bases."

Leena seemed to calm a little. "I've already told you, I left Michael at around 11pm. We had a lovely night. We discussed our future. There were no disagreements." Tears welled in her eyes.

Sloan straightened, frustrated with the lack of information thus far gleaned in the investigation. "All right, Miss Patterson, we're finished here. You're free to go."

Leena, appearing tired and emotionally frazzled, got up and shuffled to the door. As she opened it, Perez came up to her.

"Don't go leaving town," she said.

Leena just shook her head and left.

With Leena gone and the interview over, Sloan and Perez exited the interrogation room and walked down the corridor leading to their desks. Perez folded her arms.

"You believe her story?" she said.

"So far, yes. But we can't rule anyone out yet. We'll want to talk with her again before this is over."

Rounding the corner behind was Police Commissioner George Harrison, a short, rotund man with a thinning head of hair but a full, bushy mustache. He, along with Sloan, Perez and some others, was an honest cop through-and-through. Sloan and Perez, noticing him, stopped and turned around.

"I see you two are handling the Reeve case," Harrison said. "I just spoke with your captain. Any leads yet?"

"Some we're following up on, but there's still a ways to go. We haven't heard back from the lab yet for anything solid to start on," Sloan said.

"Keep on it," Harrison said sternly. "Reeve's a good cop. I'm not going to let this go unpunished. Find him or find who did this!" Harrison stalked off.

"You heard the man, Perez. We have work to do.

~ Chapter 7 ~

Michael pushed himself to the limit in the Lair's gymnasium. What started as a mere exercise in clearing his head had soon become something more. The pommel horse, the rings, the horizontal bars—Michael breezed through them with the strength and agility of an Olympic athlete.

Reaching for the towel hanging on a nearby stand, he suddenly caught sight of a familiar panel on a distant wall of the Lair. For some reason, it almost felt like there was something there, calling to him. He walked over to the wall and touched one of the panels. With a soft *click*, three sides of the panel popped open like a door. He pulled a small box out of its secret resting place. He held it gently, almost reverently, as he carried it over to a nearby desk. He opened it and saw a Rolex Submariner nestled inside. Curious, he lifted the watch out of its container.

My father's watch, he thought.

With that thought, he was instantly racked with a blinding pain in his head, much worse than the simple headache of before. Michael fell to the floor, clutching his head.

My father? Not my father! But...but...

Thoughts and images raced through his mind at breakneck speed. As though peering through a thick, milky haze, a woman's face appeared to him—it was Leena, though he didn't know her name. Then, more images—police colleagues he'd known for years, his own living room in his small apartment, Leena once more, beckoning to him sensually and enticingly. Then...

Michael snapped out of it, the pain subsiding. He sat up, wiped the pool of sweat from his brow. He had no idea what he just experienced or who those people were, but he felt an intense apprehension welling up inside him. *What on Earth was happening?* He couldn't make sense of it.

The secret door above slid open. Michael didn't know how long he'd been lying on the floor until Max was at his side. Max helped him to his feet, and steadied him.

"Are you all right, Chief?" Max asked frantically.

"It's nothing. I just stumbled," he said.

"You sure?"

Michael shot him a look which immediately told him that was the end of that conversation.

Max sighed and changed the subject. "You wanted me to alert you when it was time. Well—"

"Already?" He caught himself. "Thank you, Max. Get the car ready."

Max half-saluted, and again left him alone in the Lair. Michael couldn't believe it. Had he really been unconscious for so long? All day? Obviously he had, and that scared him.

He walked over to the many costumes lining the side wall
and removed a cowl from one of the stands. He stared at it.
It's empty, dark eyes stared back. Whatever he was going
through would have to wait. He had business tonight—with
Robert Latham.

* * * * * *

It was a cold autumn night, much colder than usual for
this time of year. A front had moved in, taking the city into
its icy grip. People milled about on the streets, bundled up,
while others were clearly under-dressed. In the poorer sections
of the city, people fared even worse. Those on the street,
especially those forced to be there, were experiencing Metro
City at its worst—with winter still to come.

There in Gladstone, an inner city borough known for its
slums and high crime, fires burned in street bins as groups of
homeless men and women huddled together, trying valiantly
to keep warm. Others, though, had other things on their
mind than mere survival.

Terry, a tall, stern and shabby-looking man in his forties,
walked down the street, past a series of bums and anyone else
courageous enough to brave these mean streets at this hour.
He scarcely looked at the people around him as he walked
with the strength of purpose in his stride. He had been told
by friends that his wife had left him and gone back to the
streets. It infuriated him and those who knew him as an
abusive, abrasive man, knew what could, and no doubt
would, happen when he was angry.

He rounded a corner, walked briskly down the grimy side
street, past more bums, then rounded another corner.

There she was, a ways down the street, standing on the
corner, hawking her wares—hawking herself. Despite the cold,

she stood there, waiting for any sad individual to pay for her services, and perhaps give her a warm bed for the night. Terry grunted and strode forward.

Maddie turned and spotted him coming toward her. The fear emanating from her was almost palpable. She turned to run, but it was slow going in those incredibly high heels. She gasped, tried to scream, but her voice was gone in the cold. An instant more, and Terry's hand gripped her shoulder. She yelped silently in pain, his grip like an iron vice. He spun her around to face him.

"Di'n't I tell ya I'd stop ya from going back on the streets? No girl a'mine's gonna be a streetwalker!" Terry barked.

"Terry, please, you're hurting me," Maddie whimpered. She was crying, which only fueled Terry's anger. He backhanded her powerfully, sending her to the pavement.

"Stop crying! Get up! You're coming home with me right now!"

Maddie got to her feet slowly, her footing clumsy in these icy conditions. Blood leaked from her cracked lip. She was still crying, but it was evident she was trying to hold it in. After all this time, after finally gaining the strength to leave him, here she was again. Nothing had changed. The circle seemed about to begin anew. And now, Terry knew, she was contemplating returning to him. She stood, and then stopped.

"No, Terry," she said, grimacing. "Do what you have to, but I'm not going back with you." she wheezed. "I'm finally free of you. I'm free in here." She patted her chest, indicating her heart.

Terry growled and raised his hand.

"Dumb bi—" A hand stronger than his own caught his arm. "Hey!"

Terry broke free and whirled to come face-to-face with The Wraith. Maddie staggered backward.

"You *are* free, now. Go," The Wraith told her, his deep, commanding voice echoing in the cold night. She turned, removed her heels, and ran as fast as she could.

"Who the hell are you?" Terry asked.

The Wraith remained silent.

"Damn you!" Angry as all hell, he took a swing at The Wraith, who merely sidestepped the attempted blow. Then, in a lightning fast move that was almost blurred in its speed, The Wraith reached out and grabbed his throat with fingers of iron, and squeezed. Terry grabbed The Wraith's arm, trying desperately to free himself. Nothing could break The Wraith's grip. The Wraith looked at his hapless victim with the eyes of a hawk ogling its prey. Terry's face reddened as he fought for breath.

"You who would prey on women. You who would raise a fist to the helpless—your days are numbered. Know now that forever more you will feel the pain you have inflicted on others, deep within you, and it is a pain that will never end to your last days on this earth," The Wraith said.

The Dread Avenger grabbed Terry by the ears. Terry sucked in the air like a diver who had been under water too long, but was too weak to resist. The Wraith brought Terry's head down into his chest and the Eyes of Judgment began to glow as The Wraith's Judgment Stare took hold.

His own scream will haunt Terry for the rest of his life!

* * * * * *

At the back of a seedy pawn shop, four punks gathered. Cox, the group's unofficial leader, rubbed his hands together, trying to rub off the cold. Donnie and Marco, the first of which carried a crowbar, moved forward toward the chained shop door.

"Okay, we all set with the plan?" asked Cox of the rest of the group. They nodded in agreement. "Then get to it!"

Marco brought the crowbar up and slid it behind the chains, searching for the perfect angle to break them. He pulled and grunted with the exertion. The chains wouldn't yield.

"Hurry up," Donnie said through gritted teeth.

"Shut up," replied Marco. "You wanna do this?"

"Shut up the both of you and get back to work," ordered Cox from behind them. He breathed into his hands, still trying to warm them. He looked up, hoping Marco was about to break the shop door's bonds, but all he saw was a terrifying silhouette against the door and shop wall. He knew the others saw it as well.

"Holy sh—!" Cox said.

"It's him," Tony said, the fourth, and messiest, of the group.

The Wraith dropped onto the group, sending them sprawling. Tony and Donnie lay there, unconscious, having bore the brunt of The Wraith's weight. Cox got to his feet, but was met by a powerful right to the chin, knocking him to the ground. Through blurred eyes, Cox watched as Marco scrambled up, and turned and ran, terrified.

* * * * * *

"This ain't happening, this ain't happening," Marco mumbled as he sprinted out of the alley and down the street. The street was more or less deserted, which suited him just fine. He didn't think he had the wherewithal to dodge any pedestrians. Not in his current panicked state.

He darted quickly round a bend, and made it to his beat-up old car. He fumbled frantically for his keys, and once inside, shoved them in to the ignition, the car gurgling to life. As fast as he could, he turned the car around and gunned the machine into the city traffic. Marco sweated buckets as he sped forward, weaving his car through the much slower traffic ahead of him.

He started to calm a little, began to breathe a little easier, when a thud on his roof startled him.

"What the he...?!" He looked up at the roof, then forward. A dark cape dropped over the windshield. "Ahhh!"

His vision blocked, he gripped the wheel tightly, trying to keep control. "Dammit."

The car swerved violently. Marco pressed down hard on the car's horn in an effort to break the traffic up in front of him. The car sped straight for the building ahead. There was no where for him to turn. His vision still hindered by that massive black cape, he sped on. The car crashed into the building at speed, a sickening clang of concrete and metal.

Marco looked up. Blood ran from a gash in his forehead, running into his eyes. He wiped the blood with his forearm, and winced in pain. He tried to open the door. It wouldn't budge. He raised his legs and kicked with as much strength as he had. The door finally yielded with a groan. He staggered out and looked around. A few onlookers were moving toward him, probably wanting to see if he was all right.

The Wraith was nowhere in sight.

Marco spotted the alley to his left and made a break for it.

Running with a limp, he was glad the alley appeared to be a short one, and he rounded the its corner narrowly.

The Wraith stood before him.

"Jesus!" Marco cried.

"He cannot help you," the grim avenger said.

It was fight or flight, and Marco took the first option. He lashed out with a right to The Wraith's head. The Wraith caught the attempted blow with ease. Marco tried again, now with his left, but the result was the same.

"Whatya want from me?" he pleaded.

"Your confession!" With that, The Wraith forced the punk's face into his chest.

* * * * * *

Detective Sloan yawned but didn't let his exhaustion stop him from continuing. He sat alone at his desk, the station minimally manned at this late hour, pouring over papers and files on the Michael Reeve case. The case had only been a day old, but that didn't matter to him. A good cop was missing.

Most likely murdered, he thought, and he wasn't going to let whomever was responsible get away with it.

Drained, he tried to rub the sleep from his eyes. His partner came toward him, looking reproachful.

"Bob, you still here? Go home. Think of your poor wife."

"In a minute. I'm trying to get things clear in my mind," he said. "What are you still doing here, Perez?"

"Unlike you, I don't have a life. Work *is* my life." She chuckled ever so slightly.

"He's gone, Perez, I just know it. Reeve's dead, and whatta we have? Squat." He shoved the papers on his desk aside. "We got nothing!"

Perez sat at the edge of his desk, looking concerned. "We've been at this all day, but it's just been one day. You expect too much too soon. Go home, get some sleep."

Sloan huffed but came to his senses. He stood and pulled his jacket from the back of his chair. "I swear I'll get who did this. Reeve was a good cop–a damn good one–and a friend. He didn't deserve the treatment he got from some of those bastards who call themselves cops here. If this is all I can do to make it up to him, I'm damn well gonna do it." Sloan was as mad as he was determined. Nothing was going to stop him.

Perez nodded. As they exited the building, Sloan eyed his partner and smiled within himself. He felt a kinship with Perez then, and knew that she would do anything, like he, to find the guilty and punish them!

* * * * * *

In the comfort of his study, Robert Latham sat contentedly at his desk, his large leather chair almost dwarfing him. He sat in silence, taking in his surroundings like a captain surveying his team. The study was opulently and eccentrically furnished. Dark timbers filled the room, but the most noticeable feature was the wall lined with the busts of some of the world's most infamous dictators–Napoleon, Julius Caesar, Joseph Stalin, Mao Ze Dong and George W. Bush, to name but a few. The phone rang, rattling him from his thoughts. He reached for the phone. The street lights glistened like twinkling stars through the large bay window behind him.

"I was expecting your call," Latham said. "Yes, everything went to plan, just as I promised you." A pause. "I assure you, Metro City is open for business. Our kind of business. Anything you want to distribute, I can handle. Yes, I can have that shipment ready for you early next week without a problem." Latham smirked. "Trust me, I took care of the Wraith. He's no longer a concern."

Right then, an explosion ripped through the window, shattering it in a fiery inferno, The Wraith leaping through almost immediately. Glass and timber rained down into the study. The Wraith landed in front of him then jumped onto the crime lord's desk, and yanked Latham up out of his chair.

"We need to talk," The Wraith said.

"It...it can't be," Latham said. "I killed you."

Gripping him by the shirt collar, The Wraith pulled him closer.

"Cease your prattling!" The Wraith said. "I want you to know, I'm watching you. Around every corner, in every empty room, *I'll* be there. And very soon you *will* be mine. That I promise you!"

The Wraith dropped Latham into his chair and leaped from the desk, through the open window, out into the frosty chill of the night.

Latham leaned back in his chair and pulled a handkerchief from his pocket. He wiped the sweat from his brow and took a deep breath.

Three of Latham's men burst through the study door, guns raised.

"You idiots!" yelled Latham, "where were you two minutes ago?"

"Hello? Hello?" came the voice through the phone's receiver. Latham grabbed the phone.

"Yes!" He waited. "It's nothing, a little accident, nothing more." He rolled his eyes. "I'll call you back, your shipment is safe, but I have more pressing concerns right now." And he hung up. Latham glared at his men. "He's alive. I don't know how, but he's alive."

~ Chapter 8 ~

Leena tossed and turned in bed. It was very late, but she hadn't slept a wink. How could she after what she'd gone through today? She sighed as she reached for the bedside lamp to her left, and switched it on. She sat up, slowly adjusting her vision to the light. In the mirror across from the bed, she looked pale and drawn, the day's events clearly taking their toll.

She remained still, trying her best to fight back the tears. She sighed again and thought perhaps she should get up and do something, anything. Sleep didn't seem to be an option right now. She slowly stood then trudged into her living room. It was average in style and size, not much larger than Michael's, but slightly better furnished, with nicer, more stylish curtains, wallpaper and carpeting–evidence of a woman's touch.

She threw a sideways glance at her answering machine. Its light was flickering. She hoped it was something that could help take her mind off things, but she knew deep down that there wasn't anything that could. Pressing the button, the automated reply chimed on with three messages.

Leena, hi, it's Astrid. Look, why not take the rest of the week off. I don't think work's the best place to be right now. Hope you're okay. We'll talk soon. Take care.

Leena wondered if work might in fact be the best thing for her, but then she realized her boss was right. She would rather mope at home than at work. She was too much of a professional to let her colleagues down or bring her personal life to the workplace.

Another message. *It's your mother, dear, call me back as soon as possible. I need to know you're okay. Oh, this silly machine. Is this recording? Hello? Call me back, dear.*

Her mother had always been a rather oppressive woman, though in the nicest possible way. Still, talking with her mother didn't appeal to her right now. She had no idea what she needed, but knew her mother couldn't help. She clicked the delete switch on the machine without listening to the last message.

She sagged into her couch, and dropped her head into her hands. The tears began to flow. She dreaded the thought of what might have happened to Michael. She hoped against hope that the police were wrong in their assessment, that Michael was okay and would somehow soon come back to her. She now realized what she had, and the thought of losing that—losing Michael—overwhelmed her. Guilt, anger and grief flowed through her in waves. She wept.

With her face buried in her hands, Leena didn't see the window to her left, let alone through it. Out into the smog-filled night, a figure on the rooftop across the street was watching, spying on her when she was at her most vulnerable. Had she been aware, had she averted her eyes in his direction, the sight would have surely chilled her. She didn't know it was The Wraith.

* * * * * *

The Wraith saw Leena, saw her crying, and he felt helpless. There was a sadness deep inside him that he'd never felt before, a feeling he couldn't explain. He tried to shake it off. He asked himself why he was here, who this woman was, and what she meant to him.

He had no answers.

~ Chapter 9 ~

Back in the Lair, Michael began removing his costume. First the gloves, then the boots and the cloak. Finally the chest piece and cowl. He placed the cowl carefully on one of the stands along the wall that housed his many costumes. He looked terrible, pained and washed out; sweat beaded his brow.

He leaned on the lab table, thoughts bubbled in his brain. Why did he feel so weak? Who was that woman? The exertion of trying to remember, of concentrating, made his constant headache feel even worse.

Max came up behind him and placed a considerate hand on his shoulder.

"You don't look so good, Chief. I don't think you should get out of bed, let alone go out again tonight," he said, concerned.

Michael looked at him sternly. He hated being mollycoddled. "I'm fine." He saw Max's expression change so softened his voice a little. "I just can't seem to shake this headache."

Max started toward the elevator. "I think you need to see Doc—"

"No!" Then, softly, "I'm fine. I just need some rest. Feels like I haven't slept in days. I'll be fine."

Max was at the elevator, looking forlorn as he pressed the switch. "Sure, have it your way." And he was up and gone.

Michael couldn't stand any longer. He dropped into the nearest chair, and rubbed his temples. It didn't help. He thought again of that lovely woman, weeping inconsolably at some obvious tragedy. While the thought of her caused him more pain, he couldn't help but doing so. Somehow, some way, she was ingrained in his psyche, and nothing he could do would drive her from there.

* * * * * *

Leena entered the Metro City Library with bleary eyes. She had slept little, and cried more. She had originally agreed with her manager's advice not to come into the library for a week or so, but the feeling of helplessness she felt at home only increased with her inactivity, and work was the only place she thought of to possibly alleviate this. She moved through the spacious lobby toward the circulation desk, and past a few of her colleagues. She ignored their concerned glances, and slipped behind the desk, making her way for the backroom staff area.

Once inside, Astrid, the Manager of Library Services, noticed her almost at once, and moved to greet her at her desk. Leena sat down and attempted to look busy, delving through the mound of paperwork which had accumulated on her desk.

"I thought I advised you to stay home," Astrid said. She was professionally, or to be more exact, impeccably dressed, with hair and makeup to match.

"I felt lost there, I needed to come and do something, be productive," she replied.

Astrid looked concerned. Leena noticed and was grateful. Leena was one of the library's best and she was well liked by all for her friendliness and professionalism. She knew, however, one look at her made it clear that she needed to be home, no matter how bad it made her feel.

"All right, we'll see how the day goes, shall we? I'm worried about you, Leena. We all are."

Leena smiled weakly, and thanked the manager for her kindness and understanding. Astrid slowly returned to her own desk, leaving Leena alone with her thoughts.

She tried; goodness knows she tried. And she even got a small amount of work done. But as the morning lengthened into the afternoon, the photo of Michael on her desk kept bringing her mind back to the realities of her situation, of Michael's kidnapping and probable murder. She managed to hold it in as long as possible, but by the afternoon, she was too tired to continue. Without one minute's sleep, she was exhausted and had to let it out. She began to cry, softly at first, but then the tears flowed. Astrid was by her side almost instantly.

"Dear, work isn't the place for you right now, I hope you realize this. The library can survive without you. You need to be home, amongst your family and friends at this time. You need their support and love. Not paperwork and patrons' problems." Astrid's voice was calm, soothing. She helped Leena to her feet, and picked up her handbag for her. "Come on, dear, I'll help you out to your car. Now please, take at least the next week or so off. I insist."

Leena said nothing, but knew Astrid was right. She allowed herself to be led toward the door.

"Thank you for all your help," Leena said, "but I can take it from here. I'll call you once...once..." She couldn't continue.

"I know, I know. I'll be in touch," Astrid said.

Leena composed herself as best she could and walked through the door, into the library proper, and toward the library's main entrance.

* * * * * *

A thick fog of steam wafted through the Metro City Men's Club sauna. A group of men, most elderly, sat in the moist heat, bulbous flesh dripping liquid, barely contained in their plush designer towels and dressing gowns.

At the far end of the sauna, in a partitioned-off section, sat Robert Latham, his head back and his eyes closed, relaxing. Alongside him to his left sat his deputy, Charlie Grieco, a slicker, more intense and younger version of Latham. Also power hungry and impatient.

"What are we doing about our problem?" Grieco asked.

Latham's eyes remained shut. "I'm taking care of it."

Grieco was agitated. "You're taking care of it? No offense Mr Latham, but—"

Latham opened his eyes and turned ever so slightly to face his deputy. "Say another word and I *will* take offense."

"Let me handle it," he said, ignoring him.

Latham put an index finger to his lips, indicating silence. It was a subtle gesture, but in this crime family, it was the strongest possible indication of Latham's anger and insistence of quiet. Grieco quieted. Latham stood.

Grieco sat idle for a moment, then followed Latham over to the curtained change area to the right of the room. As Latham dressed, Grieco prowled outside the booth like a hungry tiger, clearly still eager to push his boss.

"Then what's our plan? We're not going to sit back and let The Wraith take us down."

"What *I* have planned," said Latham impatiently, "will be made known to you in due course." He ripped open the curtains, revealing himself superbly outfitted in a very expensive Italian suit. "For now, we do nothing. I know I hit The Wraith dead center. He isn't invulnerable, of that I'm certain. Then why is he still alive? Know thy enemy, Charlie. I wish to know more before *I* do anything else."

Two armed men appeared and escorted Latham out of the sauna area and through the club he, naturally, owned.

"Enjoy the rest of your day, Charlie," Latham said with a smirk.

With his boss gone, Grieco had the freedom to brood.

Your day will come, old man, he thought. He grinned. *Your day will come, and my own future will be assured.*

With that portent of doom, he entered a booth to get dressed himself.

* * * * * *

The Metro City Police Department was a buzz of activity. Today was a busier-than-average day for crime it seemed, and the city's inadequate police force, those honest enough to do a proper day's work fighting crime, were hard pressed to make any headway. Detectives were on the phone, making enquiries by the dozen, while uniformed cops brought in a coterie of assorted perps—punks, headbangers, pimps. It was actually an awesome sight to see, and at first glance one would think this a successful day of crime prevention and detection. But considering the army of crime still out there...

Bob Sloan sat at his desk, deep in conversation on the phone. Perez came toward him with a folder. As Sloan hung up, she dropped the file on his desk.

"Got the lab results back. The blood in the apartment...it was Reeve's," she said solemnly.

"Dammit. I guessed as much, but hoped..." He paused briefly. "We still have nothing else. This isn't conclusive of anything."

"It's a start though, if nothing else. Any theories?" she asked.

Sloan leaned forward in his chair and looked grimly at his partner. "Someone Reeve once busted had a grudge and took his revenge. But, if that's the case, they did a hell of a job. There's brains behind this. This isn't just some junkie hit. But we have nothing to back any of that up."

"So what's next?"

Sloan pushed his chair back from his desk and stood. "We hit the streets. Bars, clubs, informants. Someone must know something."

Before Perez could reply, Captain Bellows shot out of his office toward the two of them.

"Okay, update time. The Commissioner's eager to know the progress on the Reeve case, even at this early stage," he said.

"Lab results are back. The blood in the apartment was Reeve's. We're definitely looking at a potential homicide here," Perez said.

"Damn. Okay, follow this through. I want to nail the bastard who did this. I'm not giving up hope that Reeve's alive, but either way, I want someone caught!"

"You and me both, Captain. We're heading out now for some food, but tonight we're going to hit everyone we know who may have some information. I ain't going home until someone tells me something," Sloan said. And with that, he stormed past Bellows and Perez, heading for the exit.

"Go with him, Perez, keep an eye on him. I know he's turning this into a personal crusade, and normally I'd step in to stop that. But I honestly think a crusade is what's needed to break this case. Keep an eye on him just the same."

Bellows slowly returned to his office, giving Perez a few things to think about.

* * * * * *

Hyde Park, in the heart of the city, was beautiful in the spring, and was one of the few areas of the city that officialdom actually funneled some money into—by way of Robert Latham's deep pockets. Latham was something of a green thumb in his spare time, and if nothing else, wanted Hyde Park to be as pristine as possible in *his* city. Flowers were in bloom, embracing the warm sunshine; trees abounded, and people were enjoying their Sunday afternoon.

Michael and Leena were strolling along the cobbled path, hand-in-hand, happy and in love. They gazed at each other, and picked a bench to sit and relax on. They kissed, appearing to all the world as the wonderful couple they were.

Then, Michael pushed her back. "Who the hell are you?" he asked suddenly. Leena stared at him in shock. Then her face blurred, as if behind a veil of mist. She appeared, impossibly, to be receding and vanishing at the same time.

Michael cried out. "Wait, I need to know who you are! Don't go. I need to find out what's going on. I need to know!"

Michael woke with a start. He was in his bed at Sanderson House, back home, his new home. He sat up and rubbed his neck, troubled by the nightmare. He still couldn't stop thinking about her; day or night, she invaded his soul. He squeezed the bridge of his nose, his headache still as strong as ever.

He bolted up and flew into his expansive walk-in-wardrobe. He needed to get out, needed some fresh air, and sitting around at home wasn't going to solve this mystery. He soon exited, dressed casually in a turtleneck, sport coat and wearing his Omega Seamaster Professional watch with the black ceramic bezel. Paul Sanderson never left the house during the day. He was a recluse, living his life only as The Wraith and nothing more. But to Michael, Paul Sanderson didn't exist. He was merely a mask for his *real* identity, and therefore served him little purpose.

Michael knew he was breaking his own rule—Paul Sanderson's rule—but there was nothing else for it. He had to find out what was happening to him, and to do that, he needed to get out.

He went into the garage. A series of classic cars shone bright before him, washed and polished to perfection. A Maserati GranTurismo Sport Automatic, Bugatti Veyron, Bufori LaJoya, Ferrarri California and several others all gleamed before him. However, his Bentley Continental GT was closest to him, and he headed straight for it, hopped inside and started the engine. It purred to life and he revved it for all it was worth.

"I have to find answers," he whispered to himself.

The automatic garage door opened. He revved the engine again.

Max raced into the garage. "Chief! Paul!"
Michael sped out and was gone in seconds.

~ Chapter 10 ~

In the impressively appointed Sanderson House kitchen, Max sat and watched Simpson hand washing the dishes. Simpson listened intently to what Max had to say, but ever the professional, didn't let that get in the way of his daily duties.

"Can't you put those in the dishwasher?" Max said.

"The master's fine bone china? Preposterous!"

Max sighed. He was stalling. He didn't want to face that something could possibly be wrong; but something clearly was.

"I'm worried. Something's gone wrong. Maybe the transfer didn't take as it was supposed to? I don't know. Something's not right. The Chief never mentioned there'd be any problems like this when he prepared us," Max said.

"Possibly. However, he remembers everything Mr Sanderson did. We have that confirmation. To all intents and purposes, he *is* Mr. Sanderson. And for us, he *must* ever be!"

"Yeah, but...I don't know. I just don't know anymore. The way the Chief laid it out, it all made sense, you know? But now, faced with the reality, faced with..."

Simpson broke him off. "Remember the vow we took? A sacred vow that can never be broken? Too much is at stake to do so."

Max looked at him. "Do you think I've forgotten? Do you think the Chief meant any less to me than he did to you?"

"Certainly not, I—"

"His death...this is killing me inside! It's all the strength I have to keep up this act, to do what the Chief wanted. To carry on his legacy. Before I met the Chief, I was a nothing, a petty thief and drug pusher in London. He turned my life around." Max paused briefly before continuing. "We both took that vow, and I will keep it 'til the day I die."

Simpson stopped, and looked at him apologetically. "I apologize, Master Maxwell. My intent was not to add to your pain nor question your loyalty, only to simply to emphasize that we must deal the hand fate his given us, as painful as it may be."

Simpson's words resonated within Max. He regained his composure somewhat. "You're right, of course. But what do we do about" —he again paused ever so slightly before continuing— "the Chief now? I tell you, something's wrong."

Faced with such a vexing question, Simpson's face clouded over in doubt. "My dear Master Maxwell, I honestly do not know the answer."

* * * * * *

It was late afternoon, and a blurred sun was arching ever lower in the sky, casting long, ominous shadows throughout the deep canyons of the city. Michael trudged down a busy street, through and around crowds of people, not really knowing where he was going, instead letting his instinct show him the way.

He crossed the street, made his way toward a familiar looking alley, and entered it. His old apartment building loomed in front of him, though he didn't recognize it as such. He looked up and saw the apartment near the top. Why was this place so familiar? Before he could do anything else, someone screamed.

"Help me!" A woman's voice, carrying so much panic that the hairs on Michael's neck stood up.

Without thinking, Michael raced off in the direction of the scream, toward the darkened alcove to the far left of the alley, which lead in turn into another larger one. He rushed down it and around a sharp bend. There, four bikers were manhandling a young lady. Dressed in garish, spiked black leather, the gang looked like it could take on an army and win. The lady was petrified and now whimpering softly. One who seemed to be the gang's leader gripped her tightly. The word "Psycho" was written across his jacket in blood-red text.

"Shuddup!" he yelled at her.

"Let her go!" Michael ordered.

Each gang member turned to face him. Normally, being faced by so many would send an ordinary person running in panic. Not the Dread Avenger of the Underworld.

"Beat it. This don't concern you," one with a purple mohawk said. The name "Chich" was written along his sleeve.

Chich stood forward, and two other bikers joined him, glaring menacingly at Michael, who stood his ground, determined. Psycho looked on with an amused expression.

"You don't hear so good!" Chich said.

"Hey, you deaf?" an unnamed biker growled.

"I said let her go!" Michael was getting impatient.

Psycho stepped forward. He tightened his grip on the young lady, causing her to yelp. "What are you gonna do? You gonna stop us? Stop us all?" He grinned through cracked, stained teeth.

Michael remained steadfast and silent.

Psycho quickly glanced at the others then nodded. The other three ran forward. Chich pulled out a set of chains, while another of the bikers produced a knuckleduster.

Chich arrived first, swung his chains at Michael's head. Michael ducked and in one fluid motion, swept out his leg, taking the biker's legs out from under him.

The other two attacked Michael from both sides. With a powerful and lightning fast spinning kick, Michael took them both out with the one blow, sending them to the ground. One was back on his feet, enraged. He screamed and lunged at Michael. Michael dodged his punches, infuriating the biker even more. He aimed straight for Michael's nose. Michael caught the blow mere inches from his face. He squeezed with fingers like steel, causing the biker to cry out in pain. The biker dropped to his knees, and Michael finished the battle with a knee to the face that shattered the hapless biker's nasal septum.

Michael whirled around at the sound of a motorcycle. Psycho, having let the poor, frightened lady go, was on his bike, revving it up for all it was worth.

"You freak!" he screamed, as he gunned his machine straight for him.

At the last moment, Michael rolled out of harm's way, and in a swift, deft motion, grabbed the chains lying on the ground and hurled them straight for the back wheel of Psycho's bike. The chains found their way into the spokes of the cycle's back wheel, slamming home in a sickening clash of wrenching metal. Psycho was torn from his seat, flew over the handle bars and landed heavily, sliding on the ground. Bleeding from wounds to the face and chest, he rolled onto his back to see Michael standing over him.

"You...ain't...human..." gasped Psycho.

Michael reached down and jerked Psycho to his feet. He held him close by the collar.

"Time to confess!" Michael growled.

* * * * * *

The Latham Industries building dominated the Metro City skyline. Over three hundred stories high, its giant "Latham Industries" logo flashed like a beacon through the night. Latham was vain enough to insist that he had the tallest building in the city, and the money and power to ensure it be so.

Deep inside the building, Latham and a series of associates were in the middle of a late night meeting, one which could very likely go for several hours more. The spacious meeting room, distinguished by the elongated table in the center of it, was filled with the thick smoke from burning cigars and pipes. Latham was seated at the head of the table and was impatient.

"All right, gentlemen, let's try and keep this meeting under control, shall we?" he said.

"It is hard to be calm, Mr. Latham, when we know that—that thing is still out there!" said the chubby Mr. Lopez who sat nearest to him.

"By thing, I assume you to mean The Wraith?" asked the skinny man beside him.

"Certainly I do. How can we do business with this...Wraith...hanging over us? It is not safe to continue as we have been. Surely we are living on borrowed time."

"Gentlemen, gentlemen," Latham said. "I do not know what else I can tell you to assure you of the safety of your orders and shipments. Despite The Wraith's continued, albeit temporary, existence in my city, it is business as usual, I promise you."

Mr. Lopez appeared more agitated than before. "How can you say this, when he just attacked you in your own home! How can you make any such assurances now?"

Seething anger began to creep behind Latham's calm visage. He kept it under control. He smiled. "Mr. Lopez, please. Everything is under control. I give you my personal guarantee on that. And you, above all, know that to be sacrosanct."

"Preposterous! I do not see how any such guarantee can be seriously made, let alone be accepted by anyone here."

Latham smiled again, this time a dangerous smile, full of malice and dread. "That is certainly your right, Mr. Lopez. Let us then cancel our business transactions, and wish each other a very good night."

He pressed a small button on the table, and almost instantly Latham's deputy, Charlie Grieco, entered the room.

"Charlie here will escort you to the next room to handle the paperwork to extricate yourself from Latham Industries. I shall be along shortly to finalize the termination," Latham said.

Mr. Lopez stood, appearing calmer and, seemingly, relieved to get out of there.

"Thank you, Mr. Latham. I will await your arrival to finish this."

Grieco led him out of the meeting room. Latham was happy, happier perhaps than he ought to have been. The remainder of the associates, twelve in total, talked amongst themselves, waiting for him to re-start the meeting.

A sickening gun-shot rang out nearby. Latham grinned.

"Ah, I believe the termination is complete," Latham said as if nothing had happened. "Now, shall we discuss the Philadelphia orders? Mr. Fubar, if you please."

The meeting proceeded.

* * * * * *

In a seedier part of town, Sloan and Perez walked toward Chico's Bar & Grill, a particularly greasy eatery, but renowned for the kinds of people who frequented it—the kind Sloan thought might have some answers in the Reeve case.

"This is the seventh place like this we've tried tonight, Bob. You think Chico'll have something for us?" Perez asked, weary. She carried a manila folder in her hand. She used it to swat a fly from her eyes.

"If he doesn't, someone else in there might. We have to at least try."

They entered. The bar was filled with the lowest inhabitants of the city—pimps, tramps, bikers, and worse. Flies swarmed above the heads of the unclean, as well as the food at the bar itself, and on the floor. The smell was of rotting food, moldy timber and body odor.

The two headed for the bar. Flashing their badges, Perez produced a photo of Michael from the folder and flashed it at the hefty, grubby bartender, Chico himself. Chico didn't seem to know Michael. Perez and Sloan moved around, repeating their enquiries to as many as they could. After several minutes, they returned to the bar, flopping onto the stools.

"We're getting nowhere," sighed Perez. "And the stink of this place." She held her nose.

"C'mon. We've seen worse than this place in our line of work. It's still early, and we have a lot of ground to cover. I'm not giving up, not by a long shot," Sloan said.

"Damn pigs!" a voice snarled to their right.

Sloan and Perez turned to face a shabby, grungy sailor-type at the far-end of the bar. He sat there with his beer, glaring at the two cops.

"What did you say?" Sloan said with a snarl of his own.

"You heard me!" was the reply.

Sloan got up, marched straight for the sailor—who was not very tall, but broad shouldered and heavy-set—and was quickly in his face. The sailor remained seated, Sloan's intimidation having no effect.

"What's your name?" asked Sloan. Perez looked on with a mixture of concern and amusement.

"What's it to ya?"

"Your name!"

"Garner. The name's Garner," he relented.

Perez joined her partner and produced Michael's photo. "You know this guy?"

"Even if I did, I wouldn't tell you," Garner grunted through what little teeth he had left. He took a swig of his beer.

Sloan was angry. "Listen, tough guy, I guarantee you, today is *not* the day to annoy me. Answer the question!"

"I don't know 'im."

He didn't believe him. He knew Garner knew something and he was determined to find out what that was.

"You sure?" he asked.

"I told you, I never seen 'im before. Now, get outta my damn face!"

Sloan gave the sailor a little shove. "Nothing would please me more."

Perez huffed. "We're wasting time here. This troublemaker doesn't know anything."

Garner snarled.

"Quiet down." Sloan shoved Garner again.

Garner grunted but remained in his seat as Perez and Sloan exited the bar.

As soon as they reached the footpath, Sloan turned to Perez. "He knows something, I'm sure of it."

"C'mon, he's just a troublemaker, out to show everyone how tough he is, how he isn't afraid of the cops," she replied.

"No. This is something more, I can feel it. He's trying to act tough, as though he knows something and won't tell us, and he thinks we can't find out. I tell you, Perez, he knows something."

"So now what?"

"We wait. Then we follow him and find out what he knows."

The two passed the time ensconced in their unmarked across the road, before Garner finally appeared at the door of the bar. The sailor, turned and lurched up the street.

"He's moving," said Perez.

"All right. Don't lose him."

They hurriedly exited their car and followed Garner, too far back for him to notice them, but close enough so they didn't lose him either.

* * * * * *

Three blocks from the bar, Garner made his way into a fleabag hotel, this one worse than most, and quickly made his way upstairs and into his room, locking himself inside.

The interior of the room was a shambles. There were holes in the floor, paint and wallpaper peeling from the walls, tiles crumbled in the kitchen and the bathroom. The furniture was sparse, and curtains, or what passed as curtains, hung in tatters from their loose hangings. Cockroaches and even a rat scurried along as Garner inched his way to the fridge for another beer. As he pulled one out, there was a knock at the door.

"Go away!" he said.

The door smashed open, and Sloan and Perez, guns raised, were inside and upon Garner before he could react. Sloan had him pinned to the floor, his arms wrenched behind him, causing him to cry out.

"Funny to find you squeamish," Sloan smirked. He quickly handcuffed the sailor. "Now we can talk in safety and privacy."

Pulling the heavy sailor to his feet, Perez again flashed Michael's photo in Garner's face. "Tell us what you know."

Garner, mortified at having been taken so quickly and easily, still wouldn't budge. "What the hell? I told ya, I don't know this guy!"

Sloan slammed his fist into Garner's stomach, winding him. "Not the answer I want to hear."

"You can't do this! You're cops. what about the law?"

"I can go all night, punk, and the law...well, right now, I *am* the law," Sloan said.

Garner coughed. "Okay, dammit, okay! They took 'im, all right? *They* took 'im."

"Who did, who took Reeve?"

"I don't know, okay, two guys dressed in black. It was dark, that's all I know. One was really tall, the other shorter, chubbier."

"Then how do you know it was Reeve they took?" Perez asked.

"The two guys walked under a lamppost as they left. They had their backs to me but the guy they carried over their shoulder...his face was in the light for a couple seconds, and it was that guy in the photo."

"Is there anything else you can tell us about those two?" asked Perez.

"It was dark. I wasn't paying close attention to them. I could barely see them. But I saw that guy," he said, again indicating Reeve.

Confusion was etched on Sloan's face. He stood back, his gun pointed at Garner. "Uncuff him, Perez. We got what we came for."

Garner rubbed his wrists once free, and reached up and grabbed his left shoulder.

"If you'd told us this in the bar, we wouldn't have had to ruin your lovely evening in this charming home of yours," said Sloan with a smirk. "We'll be watching you, Garner. Stay out of trouble!" And they left.

* * * * * *

On the street and walking back to their car, Perez looked at Sloan questioningly. "What we did back there was illegal."

"Yeah, I know," Sloan sighed, "but we weren't gonna get anything outta him unless we gave him a bit of muscle. My hunch paid off. Now we have something more to go on."

"*They* took him? Who are they? And was Reeve alive or dead when they took him? And where did they take him?" Perez had so many questions, as did Sloan. Unfortunately, neither had any answers.

Sloan knew that they were on the right track, and nothing would stop him from finding out the truth.

~ Chapter 11 ~

The door to Michael's apartment creaked open slowly. Leena slid inside, switched on the light, and closed the door behind her.

She left her handbag on the table beside the door, and dropped into an easy chair as though she had no strength left to stand. She was sad, lost.

"Oh, Michael," she whispered, "I know you're not dead, I can feel it. I can feel *you*."

She was restless and had a hard time keeping still. She stood and walked toward the sliding glass door leading onto the balcony.

"I won't leave here until you come back to me," she said. She tried to gather her strength. She had to stay positive and focused.

She slid the door open and went out onto the balcony. The crisp early evening air greeted her; she shivered as the breeze picked up, wrapping itself around her in what felt to her like a blanket of ice. She took in the cityscape then glanced down into the murky alley below.

Leena sighed, shivered again, and went back inside. She was so tired, but sleep eluded her still. How could she sleep not knowing what had happened to Michael, not knowing whether he was alive or dead? She peered into the bedroom, eying the bed. If only she could sleep...

A sharp rap on the door roused her from her thoughts. She rushed to the door, thinking—hoping—it was Michael. She opened the door—no one was there. Frustrated and a little angry, she was about to slam the door when she saw someone quickly duck around the corner at the far end of the corridor to her right. Leena stormed after them, irritated at whom she was sure was a prankster. She surely wasn't in the mood.

"Hey!" she yelled.

She now rounded the corner just in time to see a man jump into the elevator at the end of the corridor. As the elevator doors closed, the man turned to face Leena—despite the shorter hair, the bolder physique, there was no mistaking it was Michael.

"Michael?" Leena said.

She saw that the elevator was going down, and without thinking, she ran for the stairwell, leaping down the stairs two and three steps at a time, determined to beat him to the ground floor. She pushed through the stairwell door, out into the foyer, and made sped toward the elevator. The doors opened. Michael was writhing in agony on the elevator floor, clutching his head.

"Michael!" She knelt down beside him. "Michael, what's wrong?" She caressed his cheek. He didn't seem to know she was there. "Michael, can you stand? I need to get you to a doctor, the hospital." He didn't seem to hear her.

"Miss?" came an Irish-accented voice from behind them.

Leena turned to face the stranger, who was standing in the open elevator door, looking at Michael with concerned, caring, but also strangely stern, eyes.

"I'll take it from here," he said.

~ Chapter 12 ~

The Wraith leaped from one building to the next, soaring through the Metro City night, using his cape as a kind of parachute to slow his descent and to control the direction of each leap. Then, using a rope, he scaled up the side of a run-down tenement building, with practiced speed and agility. An instant later and The Wraith was off the roof and in deadly battle with three burly sailors on Metro City's docks, an unnatural fog rolling in from the Atlantic surrounding them. Just as quickly as he was on the docks, The Wraith stood atop one of the city's tallest buildings, surveying his city like a dour guard atop a prison's watchtower. The city's night-lights glistened and glittered below, somewhat pristine, even beautiful at this hour. The Wraith watched, listened...

Michael roused with a jolt, his memories of Sanderson's life as The Wraith still vivid in his mind. He was in his own bed—Sanderson's bed—back in the Sanderson mansion. He sat up, still trying to shake the cobwebs from his head. His headache was gone.

Leena sat alongside him, looking concerned and relieved at the same time. Max and Simpson were standing at the foot of the bed, the same expression upon their faces.

"Michael, are you all right?" Leena asked.

"L-Leena?" he said. His memories were suddenly coming back to him. Michael groaned a little, gripped his temples in discomfort as his true identity came flooding back—an entire lifetime returning in mere seconds. But his headache was gone, he realized again.

"Michael?" Leena touched his arm.

He let his arms drop; he was breathing easier. Whatever just happened...the discomfort—it could not really be described as pain—had subsided. He smiled weakly at her; she embraced him.

"You've come back to me, thank God!" she said with tears rolling down her cheeks.

"Leena, I..."

"I'm sorry. I'm so sorry about everything."

Michael, still coming to terms with his new-found knowledge, pushed Leena back ever so slightly.

Max came forward. "Chief, I..."

"I know the truth now, Max. I remember everything," Michael said. "I'd like to talk with Leena alone now, please. Could you and Simpson leave us?" He wasn't asking them; he was telling them.

"But..."

"Please."

Simpson, looking on with quiet dignity, placed a gentle hand on Max's shoulder, and silently persuaded the broad

Irishman to leave Michael and Leena alone to talk. When they left, Leena turned and faced him. He didn't have to read her mind to know what she was looking at—his physique. Michael had never been a wimp before, nor had he been unfit or overweight. But he never looked like this before, with a chest of steel and abs better than that of a swimwear model.

"Michael?"

He ignored her stares and began to try and explain what had only just started becoming clear in his mind. "I can't believe I'm so calm with all this. You'd think after what happened to me, I'd be ready for an asylum by now. I guess that's a testament to Sanderson's research. He knew what he was doing. The transfer worked—almost perfectly." He noticed the confusion on Leena's face and started again. "Leena, I'm sorry for what you must have gone through. All the details are only just clearing in my own mind. I'm still trying to take this all in; it's awesome to say the least. And you know the funny thing? I'm not really mad."

Michael stood and began to pace alongside the foot of the bed.

"Michael, tell me what's going on. Why do you look so different? What's happened to you, where have you been?"

"I'll tell you everything. You deserve that and so much more." He sat next to her. "That was Max Horton and Jonathan Simpson, my associates."

Leena looked at him with surprise. "Your...associates?"

Michael sighed. This was harder than he thought. "They're Paul Sanderson's staff."

"I figured that. We're in his house after all," she said.

"They're Paul Sanderson's staff, and I'm...well, I'm Paul Sanderson!" He paused briefly. "And The Wraith!"

Leena's eyes widened. "I don't understand any of this, you're Michael Reeve, not—" She stood.

"I'm both of those men. Leena, something happened to me the night I disappeared, something amazing, something even I can't truly understand, and now I'm both the recipient and the instigator of this whole thing." He got up as well. He was still amazed at what happened to him. "Sanderson was also The Wraith. He's real. The urban legend is real, and always has been. Somehow, someway, I—Sanderson—passed everything on to me. His powers, his memories, emotions—everything. In almost every sense of the word, I *became* Paul Sanderson."

"No. I won't accept that. I can't."

"I *am* Paul Sanderson, as much as I am Michael Reeve."

He didn't know what else to do but tell the truth.

"I don't know what to think about all this, I don't know what to believe." After a pause, she said, "How can you say all this? How can you be so calm about the whole thing? These people tried to steal your life!"

Michael attempted to reach out to her, but she stepped back further. "I know I should be furious at the least, emotionally disturbed at worst. But I'm not. I have Sanderson's memories and emotions. For all intents and purposes, I *am* Sanderson. I know what it's like to fight for the greater good, to make those kinds of sacrifices. I know and understand that what he did, despite all the pain it caused, was the right thing. At least as he saw it." He paused to catch his breath, and saw the pain and sadness in Leena's eyes. "I know how this must hurt you, and I'm sorry to lay all this on you at once, especially now. But you need to know everything, you need to know the truth, and my telling you now is helping me make sense of things as well." He had to make her believe, had to make her accept what happened. "I was part of my—Sanderson's—backup plan. If anything were to happen to me—to him—" It was almost impossible to distinguish between himself and Paul. "He chose me as his successor. This is so weird, Leena. I'm having trouble with this myself. I can remember it all firsthand. Because of my lack of a family, and the kind of person I am, my belief in The Wraith, my lifelong wish to help people—he chose me to become him! The research I—he did—was incredible." He turned away from her, dropped his head. "And now I'm..."

She pulled him around to face her. "You're Michael Reeve, the man I love more than anything in this world."

"But I'm so much more now, Leena. I'm two men at once."

Leena placed her hands on his chest, tears welling in her eyes. "I didn't know what I had until I lost it...lost you. I love you so much. I want you back. I need you."

Michael wished he could take her pain away. For all his abilities, his intelligence, his resources, that seemed the one thing he was incapable of, and it pained him to see her like this. But he couldn't deny what had happened no more than he could reject his destiny.

"I love you too, but it's not as simple as that. This isn't some soap opera. I've changed. I can't go back to what I was, to what we were. And I can't ask you to come with me where I must go, on the journey I must take."

Leena wiped her eyes, but the tears kept coming. "What are you saying?"

"I can't believe how clear this is in my mind, but...Michael Reeve is dead. To all the world, that is the case, and must remain so. I'm sorry."

"I can't believe what I'm hearing!"

Though it pained him, he was determined to lay it all out before her. He loved her more than a human being could possibly love another, but he had more to think about than just himself as Michael Reeve. He couldn't change what had happened to him, and he knew there was more for him to do. The fact he loved Leena so much was what gave him the strength to spare her the sacrifice she would have to make to be with him. He had to spare her that.

"I'm sorry," he said softly.

Leena fell on the bed, crying. Michael felt terrible. Was he doing the wrong thing? He yearned to take her in his arms, tell her everything was okay, that they'd work it out, but the Paul Sanderson half of him knew better, knew it couldn't be. Conflicted, aching, he couldn't bear to watch anymore, and retreated from the bedroom, thinking it best to leave her alone.

~ Chapter 13 ~

Max paced nervously in the kitchen, while Simpson, ever cool and calm, tried to continue with his daily chores. He stopped and looked up at Max.

"Must you do that, Master Maxwell?" he asked, raising an eyebrow.

"I can't help it. I can't help thinking what must be going down up there. This could be the end of everything."

"Would that truly be so bad? Master Sanderson had paid his debt to society, done more than any one man ever had, would ever be expected to do. Now that his plans seem to have failed, do we really have the right to keep Mr. Reeve from his real life?"

"But it can't just die with the Chief. It has to go on. So much can still be done, needs to be done, not just in this city, but this hell-hole we call a world." He sighed. "It can't just die like this."

The rising noise of a car engine revving in the nearby garage silenced them. Max just had time to peer out the kitchen window, managing to catch a glimpse of the Bentley Continental GT screeching down the drive, past the gardens.

"There he goes again," Max said with a heavy breath. He glanced at his watch. "Damn. He's switched the tracker off. Then—"

"He still has Master Paul's memories," Simpson said.

"Holy—What does that mean? Where's he going?" Max asked, even though he knew Simpson couldn't answer him.

"You tell me," said Leena, standing in the kitchen doorway, her eyes red from crying, her face tense with fury.

* * * * * *

Back in his old neighborhood, Michael surveyed his apartment building—and remembered. He had only been living as Paul Sanderson for a few days but it felt like a lifetime had passed. He now had the complete lifetime experiences of two very different yet inexplicably similar men inside of him, and while he was beginning to make sense of the senseless, those memories still jumbled around in his brain. He looked to his Omega watch. It was late afternoon.

"Arrgghh!" he screamed. "What should I do? How can my life, my purpose, be so clear and so muddled at the same time?" A rhetorical question, for deep down he knew exactly what needed to be done, but that didn't make the decision any easier, and he hated having to hurt the love of his life because of it. He saw no alternative, however. He slammed the bottom of his fist against the building in frustration. "Sanderson knew what he was doing, but somehow the process was flawed. I wasn't supposed to remember my past life. But I do." Talking out loud seemed to help clear things up somehow.

He kicked an empty soda can along the ground and disappeared around the corner of his former home.

* * * * * *

Night had fallen, and The Wraith had replaced Paul Sanderson, out patrolling his city. He thought perhaps hitting the streets would help clear his head further. It always used to, at least, for the real Sanderson it had. The *real Sanderson*. How strange the thought was. Perched amongst a series of hideous gargoyles on a roof's edge, he pondered his situation and knew there was no escape. He prowled the shadows behind the gargoyles, attempting to gain a better vantage point, when a woman's blood curdling scream shocked him from his thoughts. He tapped at his temple and infra-red lenses slid down into place over his eyes; an invention of Max's. He tried to ascertain the direction of the scream. There, a distance away, down in the alley, he could see two bums standing over a man and woman lying on the ground. The Wraith silently dropped over the building's side, falling into the inky abyss.

At street level, the two bums scowled at their prey. Both were outfitted in dirty, ill-fitting rags. One had a beard which seemed to hold more food in it than his belly; the other had long hair barely contained by a tattered beanie. The bearded lout leered with nicotine and plaque-stained teeth.

"Di'n't hafta be this way. We just wanted yer cash an' that necklace," he said.

"C'mon lady!" ordered the other one. He took a step toward her.

The woman was too terrified to respond. She merely whimpered over her husband's unconscious form. The bum with the long hair reached inside his pocket and pulled out a rusty switch-blade.

"Don't make me get rough," he said. The knife's blade flicked out from its handle.

The woman slowly reached inside her husband's inner jacket pocket, presumably searching for his wallet. Even from where The Wraith watched, he could see her hands trembling. He came up behind them. "Why don't you try *me* for size."

The bums spun around. The Wraith's Eyes of Judgment glowed an incandescent yellow, shimmering demonically.

"Oh. My. God," breathed the bum with the beard. He turned and ran, having caught religion immediately and fearing for his life.

The Wraith slowly walked toward the one with long hair, who held his switch-blade up, waving it about.

"I advise you to stop now," said The Wraith.

The bum sneered, tossing the knife from one hand to the other in a pathetic display of bravado. "I ain't gonna let some costumed freak scare me!"

The Wraith stood tall and upright, his cape wrapped around him. The bum took a swing with his knife, but he wasn't close enough for The Wraith to even flinch. He stepped closer, swung high, The Wraith ducking under the attempted blow. The bum then went for a gut shot, but The Wraith caught his arm, and forced the knife from the thug's grip. The bum cried out. The Wraith delivered a powerful blow to the bum's stomach, winding him badly, forcing him to his knees.

The Wraith grabbed him by the hair, lifted him back to his feet, and pulled the bum's face toward his chest. With this effort, the Eyes of Judgment took hold.

"Feel the pain of your victims. Feel the guilt that is rightfully yours," The Wraith intoned.

It was over in seconds, with the bum slumping to the ground unconscious, sleeping temporarily before waking to a lifetime worth of pain and anguish, a life in which he would forever attempt to make good for his past crimes. But The Wraith was no longer interested in him. He turned back toward the cowering woman, who seemed just as afraid of him as she was of her attackers.

The Wraith approached her slowly, not wishing to frighten her even more. "Are you all right, Miss?" he asked in a voice much lighter and softer than usual. It was Michael's voice, not The Wraith's. "Are you all right?"

"I...you're..." the woman started.

The Wraith knelt before her, being mindful to remain gentle.

"I won't hurt you," he spoke softly. He glanced at the woman's still unconscious husband.

"My husband...he's been hurt," she said.

"It's nothing serious, though I'll call an ambulance to be sure," he said.

The woman seemed to finally calm a little, and gave him a tired smile . "Thank you," she said softly. She looked down at her husband. "I don't know how to..."

But The Wraith had vanished.

* * * * * *

The Wraith had returned to his perch amongst the gargoyles. He watched intently as the police and an ambulance, as well as a small crowd of onlookers, had congregated on the street below. He was soon again consumed by his thoughts.

He'll be okay, he thought. *A crack on the head won't do him any lasting damage.* His thoughts wandered. *Metro City. A hothouse of evil. But good people still live here. The city needs me. Am I not its protector?*

He continued to watch the proceedings below.

* * * * * *

Back at street level, an ambulance officer pushed the gurney with the woman's husband up into the ambulance while she stood alongside and watched.

"He'll be all right," the medic reassured her. "Minor head wound and concussion. We're taking him to City General to check him out." He shut and latched the double rear door.

A police officer approached the woman. Behind him, the bum who attacked her was being led away in handcuffs.

"Now, Mrs...Jones?...let me get things straight. You say two people attacked you and your husband while you were walking to your car, but one of the attackers got away. And then...The Wraith came and saved you?" The officer was reading from his notebook. It seemed he was trying to keep a straight face.

"He appeared from nowhere, saved our lives," she said.

"Right," the officer said sarcastically. He turned to face a colleague standing nearby, and pulled a face, indicating his thoughts of the woman's state of mind. She noticed, but didn't care.

"Can I go now? I want to be with my husband."

"Of course. We're through here, Mrs. Jones. I'm sorry."

* * * * * *

Up on the roof, The Wraith smiled.

I'm needed here, he thought. *No matter who I am, Metro City needs me, the people need me—need The Wraith. I know what my destiny is and I know what my decision must be.*

~ Chapter 14 ~

With a renewed vigor and sense of purpose, The Wraith spent the rest of the night launching into action, combating evil wherever he found it, moving through the night like a avenging spectral force. He stopped an attempted burglary, busted a drug deal, engaged in deadly combat with some gun runners near Metro City harbor. Later, back in the city, The Wraith dealt with a sadistic pimp, then proceeded to help a hooker to her feet, her lip beginning to swell after having been beaten up.

He watched from the safety of the shadows as police officers, detectives and crime lab personnel worked over a murder scene on one of the city's many side streets. He tackled an attempted rapist, he having reached the scene in the nick of time to prevent a horrible crime. In an abandoned warehouse, muddy footprints led to a gang of kidnappers. He even found the time to bust a safe-cracker when he cracked open the safe of one of the city's wealthiest citizens.

At the end of a very busy night, The Wraith again found himself on his perch, joining his "friends," the gargoyles. It was very early morning, but the sun had yet to rise, and wouldn't for another hour or so. He would be long out of the city by then, back home.

'Home.' Such a strange word now, he thought. It was and it wasn't at the same time. Yet, he knew what must be and what he must do to make things right.

* * * * * *

The warehouse district of Metro City was known for its old, decrepit structures. Less than half of the buildings in the area were still in use, and those that weren't were invariably in various states of disrepair. Some were outright structurally unsound. Organized crime, indeed crime of any sort, found in this neighborhood a sanctuary for their nefarious activities and almost anything of vice could be found here. Almost anyone could be found for any job...for a price.

Behind a dilapidated warehouse, Robert Latham entered the grim, imposing alley, holding his nose as he walked. Surrounded on either side by massive walls of rotting timber, he made his way uneasily along the path. The alley itself was scattered with debris—trash, boards, shingling, old posts, all of which added to the atmosphere of disorder and decay. He'd been in the area before, several times, most recently when he had to take personal action against The Wraith, for all the good it ended up doing him. But, he always did it as a last resort. It was careless for him to be potentially seen here, but when action required his own personal touch, he was there when needed. He felt he was needed now.

The early morning chill bit through Latham's leather-gloved hands. He pulled his collar up over his neck. He looked around and waited. There was the crunch of gravel behind him, but he didn't immediately turn.

"Thank you for agreeing to see me on such short notice," Latham said calmly. "I'd like to—"

The stranger interrupted him but remained shrouded in the darkness at the far end of the alley. "How did you find me?" he asked in a raspy voice, deep and powerful.

"I have my ways. Let's leave it at that."

The stranger stepped forward but still remained in the shadows. His immense frame, however, was something he couldn't hide. He was massive, almost seven feet tall, and as broad as a wardrobe, Latham estimated.

"I know why you contacted me—The Wraith," the stranger said.

"You're the only one I know of who can get the job done. Many have tried and failed. Even myself, though I could have sworn otherwise."

"It will cost you."

"Anything. Just get rid of The Wraith. Do anything it takes to take him down!" He took a breath. "I...I heard you two may have some...history together..."

The stranger huffed. "Anything?" He shuffled where he stood, obviously relishing the thought of what he had just been offered. "I will do as you ask but for myself, not for you. And once the job is complete, I will take what is mine."

Latham grew uncomfortable. He rarely worried. Why should he now? Despite The Wraith's causing him problems at times, he was still the master of Metro City. But the thought of the figure behind him taking what he wanted—the city, for all Latham knew—chilled him to the bone.

"Yes, I know this...Wraith. I know him," the stranger said.

"Well then—" he began. It was too late. He was alone, the stranger having vanished. Latham stepped forward, stood where the stranger had been only seconds earlier, and wondered how he had managed to disappear so suddenly and so silently. The chill in the air seemed to suddenly have an extra bite to it.

~ Chapter 15 ~

The morning sun crept through the blinds of the Sanderson library. It had been a long, excruciating night, and Leena and Max were still arguing, Leena's energy fueled by her anger, directed mainly at Max, who wasn't as sympathetic to her plight as he perhaps might have been. Simpson watched silently.

"How could you do this to Michael? To us?" she said.

Max tried to rub the tiredness from his eyes. He looked exhausted and Leena felt sure she had made him feel more uncomfortable than he was used to feeling. She liked that. She *wanted* to get under his skin.

"Miss," Max started. "Look, I truly am sorry, believe me, I am. It's what the Chief wanted. Under the circumstances—tragic circumstances I might add—we all thought it was for the best."

"To steal another man's life?"

Max threw his hands up. They had been over the same ground all night. Leena knew nothing would be resolved; they both clearly had different points of view. But after days of anguish, now was the time to let it out, and Max was the available recipient of her rage.

Max flopped onto the comfortable wing chair.

"I shall brew a fresh pot of tea," said Simpson.

"You go do that," Leena said. As Simpson left, she now stood before Max, trying her best to be as intimidating as she possibly could.

"Miss, if only you'd try to understand. This isn't just one man we're talking about here, but a legacy! A lasting legacy that can do so much good. We couldn't just let that end with the Chief's death. It had to go on!"

"You mean The Wraith?" she queried.

"Yes, Leena," came Michael's voice. "The Wraith."

* * * * * *

The secret door from the Lair had only barely opened, but Michael managed to catch on to what Leena and Max had been talking about. And one look at their faces confirmed to him how long the conversation had been taking place. Michael stepped into the library, and the secret door slid back into place with a soft whirring of gears.

Leena quickly embraced him, grabbing him tightly, not wanting to let him go. He couldn't help but return the embrace. He wished he could do so much more.

"Thank you, Max. I'm sure she's been quite a handful tonight. I need to talk with Leena alone now though," Michael said.

"Sure, please do," Max said, obviously relieved.

With Max now gone, he carefully led Leena over to the wing chair, and gently sat her down. "I have to say this now or I never will. I can't give this up, Leena. I've thought about this all night. I've seen the good that is done with the abilities I possess. This is my destiny. To help people, those who can't help themselves. That's always what my life has been about, hasn't it?"

Her eyes seemed to plead with him. "But you don't need to be someone else to do that. You *were* doing that as Michael Reeve!"

He found it hard to look her in the eye, so turned away before speaking. "Not in the same way, not as effectively. I can't ignore what I've become, what I can now do. For this to work, to truly work, I must become, and remain, Paul Sanderson." She gasped. "If you only knew the things I now know, the things I now see...I just wish I could put those things into words."

Leena stared blankly, clearly not knowing what to think. She'd been through so much the last few days, Michael knew, experienced more pain than anyone could or should ever have to. His heart bled for her.

She stood firm, now looking more determined than hurt, and put a hand to Michael's shoulder, forcing him around to face her. "I just want the man that I love back." Her eyes filled with tears.

"He's...I'm here, but...but I must be Paul Sanderson now, as much as I know that hurts you. I have to do this." He took a deep breath. "My life is sworn to justice. I can't ask you to stay with me; that's too much to ask of anyone, that's too much of a sacrifice for you to make."

Leena was clearly frustrated, and a little angry. "You said that to me before. How dare you make those decisions for me! You don't have to ask me anything. It's not your decision to make. I've been thinking tonight as well, not to mention the last few days. I've had time to do little else." She, too, took a deep breath. "I'm not going anywhere."

Michael took a step back. This wasn't what he expected to hear, this wasn't the Leena he remembered. "You can't. This isn't the life for you. This isn't a life of luxury or of comfortable living. You deserve so much better, so much more than pain and heartache."

"Would you stop trying to rule my life! Those aren't your decisions to make, Michael. I just got you back. I won't lose you again." Michael tried to interject, but Leena stopped him. "Despite the pain I've been through, I think I've grown as a person. I've grown up. I know now what I had, and how I should have cherished that. I don't care what you call yourself; I don't care what you do. I can't say I fully understand what's going on here, or why you're doing this. We have a lot to sort out and talk about, but if this is the life you're now determined to lead, then I want to be a part of it. I need to be. If Max and Simpson can join you in your mission, so can I."

Every reason Michael previously thought of to turn her away didn't seem to matter anymore. He found himself melting in her presence. He loved her deeply, that had never changed, never faltered. His previous reasoning didn't seem to make sense anymore.

"I don't know what to say," he finally said.

Leena moved closer. Michael briefly considered pushing her away, but he fought the Sanderson part of him back. They embraced, and kissed. After what seemed an eternity, they broke.

"Leena, if you're serious about this,
he said, "then there have to be some changes. I'm different.

For this life you've chosen, to live in this world, *you* have to change as well."

Leena looked troubled, as he reached into his pocket, and removed a small remote control device. He pressed the button and the bookshelf—the secret door—slid open again.

"Come with me," he said, as he turned and strode through the darkened passageway.

Inside, with Leena by his side, he switched on the light, revealing the Lair. Bathed in a series of powerful overhead lights, the Lair's awesome presence weighed on the both of them. He watched as she tried to take in her surroundings. She stepped forward and looked up, the ceiling which seemed to belong inside of a vast, man-made subterranean grotto stared back. The expansive ceiling curved down on the sides, blending into metal walls, futuristic and impressive in design and structure. It was unlike any building or room she had ever seen before, Michael knew.

Below them was the crime lab, banks of computers, the gym and more. Her expression of wonder spoke volumes.

"This is where I work, where I train, where I heal. This is my refuge," Michael said, following her as she stepped further in.

He then ushered her onto the elevator pad, and activated it. As they slipped quietly down, he noticed her eyes settle on the wall lined with at least a dozen or so Wraith costumes, all perfectly placed on individual stands, ready whenever they were needed.

"Lord," she said.

She remained on the platform while Michael went to the gymnasium on the opposite side of the Lair.

"This is where you'll be spending most of your time, at least to start with," he said.

Leena joined him. "Excuse me?" she asked.

"My world is filled with danger," he said. "To be a part of it, you have to be willing and ready to face those dangers, and be physically able to do so. To join me in my quest, you have to be able to assist me, whenever I may need you."

Leena began to look troubled, and Michael knew she was beginning to let self doubt creep in. It was an awesome undertaking he was proposing to her. He wasn't just asking her to work out a little, like some pumped up movie star preparing for a specific role. He was basically telling her she needed to be his equal; he needed to be able to count on her at all times.

"I...I'm not sure that I can," she said.

"I'll train you, help you every step of the way. It will be tough, and you will want to back out. But you won't go through this alone, I promise you. You can do this. That's the one condition you must keep."

Leena looked determined. "You're right, I *can* do this. I'll prove to you I can."

He smiled, took her hands in his, gave them a peck. She eyed the gym equipment, presumably readying herself to begin her own quest, one Michael knew would be difficult, filled with pain, sweat and tears. There was no turning back now. He felt satisfaction on one hand, trepidation on the other. *Was he doing the right thing?* He mused over this question while Leena began slowly familiarizing herself with some of the gym's equipment. He knew what his own destiny would be, and now with Leena...well, he didn't think life would ever be boring.

~ Epilogue Part 1 ~

In his darkened study, Robert Latham sat for a long while at his desk, brooding. Eventually, he placed his elbows onto his desk, resting his chin on his thumbs. He was pensive, irritable.

"He's coming now," he whispered. "God help those who get in his way."

~ PART 2 ~

PART 2

~ Chapter 16 ~

It was a full six months of intense training before Michael, now forever more known to the world—and to himself—as Paul Sanderson, declared Leena fit to work by his side; another four months before he allowed her to move in with him in Sanderson House, the palatial home to the Sanderson family for generations, to publicly announce their "new" relationship. During those ten months, Leena "mourned" for Michael, who had ultimately been declared dead, and then after a suitable length of time, was swept off her feet by the reclusive millionaire Sanderson, who had decided to slowly come back into the public eye after years of shying away. While the original Sanderson eschewed a personal life—choosing his mission as The Wraith to be his life—the new Sanderson had other ideas. His life's mission, born from the memories of the deceased original Sanderson's life and travels, was intact and as strong as ever, but he was determined to live and love at the same time, now that Leena was forever a part of his new life.

These ten months were also difficult. While Paul's personal life was once again fulfilled, and he took to his new life's work as The Wraith as though he was born into it, a new menace had infiltrated not only Metro City, but large tracts of the country as well. Hundreds of men, possibly thousands—the figures in the news reports were never clear—had gone missing. Many of the them were men who had little contact with the outside world. They were those who had little or no family, or because they had seen better days, or were the homeless and destitute. Police had been investigating for months but without success. No clues were ever found, no sign of the men ever seen.

The Wraith joined the hunt early on, but he too had been stumped by the mystery, and this troubled him greatly. Those of the homeless deemed too weak or elderly were viciously slaughtered, and while The Wraith had been able to confront one of those responsible, someone calling himself Magnus Khan, he had been unable to stop him, which troubled him even more. It was clear Khan was acting on the orders of someone else, someone truly powerful, but as to that person's identity and purpose, that remained a mystery. In the end, he had little more answers than the authorities. As the weeks dragged on into months, The Wraith grew ever more frustrated and desperate for answers.

Another two months passed.

* * * * * *

It was a mild October evening and people streamed through the grounds of the Latham estate. It was dark and the people were loosely dressed to take advantage of the unseasonably warm weather. Robert Latham was holding a benefit dinner for his own cancer foundation, and all the city bigwigs and power brokers had been invited. It was a classy affair, with the many men outfitted in expensive black tie fashions, while on the women, impressive jewelry sparkled in abundance.

Paul Sanderson's classic Daimler sedan rolled up the drive and stopped before the large home's front entrance. Paul and Leena exited the car and Max waved them off before they made their way slowly up the impressive path toward the house. Leena looked lovely, Paul thought, in a flowing, stylish Prada gown, her body now more sculpted, reflecting her past twelve months of training. Paul tugged at his collar uncomfortably. He needed a new tailor. But more than that, being there made his skin crawl.

"Anything wrong, darling?" Leena asked.

"Being here, in the lair of the devil, pretending."

Robert Latham and the reach of his evil empire made Paul's blood boil. On the surface, he was a respected businessman, employer of thousands and generous supporter of charities, his own or otherwise. Very few knew the truth—that Robert Latham was the head of the biggest crime syndicate on the eastern seaboard, dealing in drugs, weaponry, even stolen cars. And he was the power behind the power in Metro City. His syndicate was the intricate weavings of a spider's web, with Latham himself the horrendous spider at its center—in control, insidious, deadly.

Paul and Leena made their way through the throng of people inside the house, smiling and greeting people here and there, before arriving in the spectacular ballroom, the main hub for the night's festivities. A large, ornate crystal chandelier hung above them and the room was richly decorated and furnished throughout. Scanning the room,

Paul recognized the Mayor, Police Commissioner George Harrison and other prominent officials and citizens.

And Robert Latham, who was moving toward them.

"Evening, Sanderson, good to see you," Latham said with a lascivious smile. "I'm overjoyed the both of you could make it. Your support of this very worthy cause is, of course, very much appreciated."

Leena smiled. "Thank you, Robert."

"Well, cancer research is indeed a worthy cause, Robert. We wouldn't be anywhere else tonight," Paul said with as much charm as he could muster. When he wanted to, he could lay it on thick, and very naturally, without a hint of falseness.

"You've done so much already. This party just caps it all off so wonderfully," Leena added with a friendly smile.

Latham, as vain as he was intelligent and calculating, smiled coolly, drinking in the praise and apparent admiration. With a casual wave, he began to move away, returning to the crowd. Paul was glad to see the back of him.

"Mingle, enjoy the night," were Latham's parting words before he was meeting and greeting someone new.

"Now that he's preoccupied, I can start to look around," Paul whispered to Leena. "Keep an eye on him."

"Be careful, darling," she whispered back.

Paul, hands in his pockets, went over toward the large double-doors at the opposite end of the ballroom. Upon reaching it, he turned, checking subtly if anyone was watching him. A nod from Leena the coast was clear, and he quickly ducked inside the door.

Latham had managed to keep things, while not exactly on the straight-and-narrow, certainly much lower key in recent months, and Paul had to find out what he was up to. The cancer charity gala tonight was the perfect excuse for a little snooping around Latham's home. Latham was well known for conducting much of his business at home, and Paul knew if there was something to find, Latham's study would be the likely place.

* * * * * *

Leena was standing alongside the double-doors, still in the ballroom, sipping from a particularly fine glass of Armand de Brignac champagne. She was nervous, but didn't let it show. The Latham house being so filled with people increased the risk for Paul, or so she thought, but Paul decided the operation was worth that risk. As she turned this over in her mind, Commissioner Harrison greeted her.

"Hello, Leena, lovely to see you again. Paul not with you tonight?"

"Oh, he's off checking on the car," she lied. "Enjoying the party, Commissioner?"

"As much as I can at this sort of thing." Harrison looked as uncomfortable now as Paul had earlier. "Leena, I...I still can't get over how much Paul looks like Michael. I mean, they're almost identical, and yet...they're not. I know that makes little sense, but—"

Leena stopped him, knowing what he was about to say. She'd heard it before. "You don't have to say it...we've been through this before. It's been a year now. Michael's gone, and I've moved on. It's been a tough year, but I'm happy again. Paul came into my life, and...I'm happy again."

Harrison looked at her with an almost fatherly expression. "I'm sorry, my dear, you're right. I just hate that we were unable to find his...well..." He glanced downward. "Michael would be so proud of you."

Leena was touched by this, and almost wished she could let Harrison in on the secret. Through a strange twist of fate and circumstance, he had become another man, taken on another life, and was now all the better for having the best parts of two very fine men. Only herself, Max Horton, their comrade and resident inventor, mechanic and chauffeur; and the faithful butler, Jonathan Simpson, knew the truth. And it had to stay that way.

She flashed a shy smile at Harrison. "Thank you."

Harrison held her hand and the moment was a warm one. He then seemed to see someone else he wished to talk to. "Excuse me, my dear."

Leena raised her glass to him and he left her. She was worried about Paul. No word yet from him—though it hadn't been long—and she wondered if he had found anything of interest.

* * * * * *

After having ducked through the double-doors, Paul found himself in a lengthy corridor. By his estimate, having researched his enemy's stronghold long ago, Latham's study should be at the end, so he moved in that direction. Reaching the door to the study, Paul listened to see if anyone was inside. Latham was still in the ballroom and there was no other way into the study, and not a sound came from within. He gripped the solid gold handle, and inched the door open. It was dark inside, but not completely pitch, as the estate lights shone slightly through the large bay window at the back of the room.

Paul squeezed inside and shut the door quietly. He briefly wondered where to look first, before his thoughts were abruptly stopped by the dreadful sight before him—a woman's body lying on the floor. She was young, pretty, and while there were no immediate signs of violence on the body that he could see, he nevertheless could tell she was dead, not merely drunk or passed out.

Paul knelt by the body and checked for a pulse. Dead. In the minimal light, he now recognized her as Barbara Latham, Robert's twenty-five-year-old daughter. The body was still warm—she hadn't been dead long.

There were no wounds or marks of any kind on the corpse.

Who would want to kill Barbara Latham? he wondered. *And why? To get to her father? An obvious choice,* he realized. Perhaps too obvious.

Standing, he just made out in the corner of his eye an object lying on the floor. Using his handkerchief to pick it up, he read the label on the small cylinder—Tavelli Cosmetics. It was an expensive brand of lipstick, the kind fashionable and wealthy young women like Barbara used the world over. Thinking it a possible clue, he pocketed it, just as the sound of people approaching the study came from behind the door.

"Senator Babcock, please," came the distinct voice of Robert Latham. "Let me just get the figures from my study and I'll prove it to you."

Seeing nowhere to hide, Paul knew there was no excuse acceptable for being in Latham's study with the body of his daughter, so he made the only decision possible—he made a dash for the bay window. Just as the door to the study began to open, Paul leaped for and through the window, shattering it in an explosion of glass.

* * * * * *

"What the...?" Latham shouted as he entered the room. He saw the smashed remains of the window, but saw too the lifeless body of his daughter. He fell to her side, took her body in his arms and screamed.

Senator Babcock, a stocky, white-haired gentleman, rushed in.

"Oh no," the Senator uttered in shock.

"It was The Wraith, it was him," Latham said as he clutched poor Barbara's body, rocking her in his arms.

A large crowd began to build at the study door, the noise of the breaking window and Latham's cries startling them in the ballroom. Commissioner Harrison barged his way through the crowd and attempted to take charge of the situation.

He tried to push the crowd from the door. "Back, please, everyone. This is a possible crime scene, please step back."

Hopelessly outnumbered, Harrison was saved by a band of Latham's men, six of them, who helped him in clearing the crowd and leading them back to the ballroom.

"Make sure they all stay in the ballroom. No one is to leave," Harrison told one of Latham's men, who nodded in agreement. Harrison then quickly marched back to the study.

* * * * * *

The large crowd in the ballroom buzzed with excitement, anger and fear. Leena was worried, and scanned the crowd for any sign of Paul. She turned to her right. Nothing. To her left, and Paul was casually standing alongside her.

"I just made it out of there in time. I'm certain Latham didn't recognize me," Paul whispered in her ear.

"I'm sorry. Latham and the Senator rushed in, I didn't have a chance to stop them or warn you," Leena admitted. "What's going on in there?"

"Latham's daughter is dead. Murdered. Before I was interrupted, I did manage to find" —he removed from his pocket the small lipstick, just enough for Leena to see— "this." He put it back in his pocket.

"Lipstick?" Leena queried.

"We need to get this to the lab as quickly as possible. We'll have to slip out of here before the police arrive en masse."

"Commissioner Harrison ordered Latham's men to keep everyone inside the ballroom."

Paul smiled at her and began to lead her through the bustling crowd. "I wouldn't worry about that."

With that, they disappeared from sight.

~ Chapter 17 ~

Latham sat, stone-faced in a smaller, but no less opulent, room. Charlie Grieco stood beside him, looking agitated, ill at ease with the company he now kept. On the other side was Latham's attorney, Rupert Gough, a tall man in his fifties with silver-grey hair, appearing calm and dignified. Commissioner Harrison and Detectives Sloan and Perez were also present.

"Are you sticking with your story, Mr. Latham?" Sloan asked.

"My client has given you a full statement, gentlemen," Gough said tersely.

Latham spoke up. "It was The Wraith, damn it. I saw him. He escaped through the window, he—he murdered my daughter!"

Sloan looked at Latham and tried to think of just how to tell him The Wraith didn't exist. "Mr. Latham, I just can't accept what you're saying. The Wraith? He's just an urban legend, a bogeyman to scare people. I just can't—"

"Are you insinuating that my client has lied in his statement? I certainly hope not," Gough said.

"Well, I just can't—" Sloan said, before Harrison broke him off.

"I think that's enough, Sloan, Perez. If we need to speak with Mr. Latham again, I'm sure he'll be only too happy to co-operate." Harrison indicated the door with a nod. He faced Latham. "Excuse us."

The three police officers congregated in the corridor outside. Sloan gave Harrison a sharp look, but said nothing.

"You don't buy that story do you?" Perez queried.

"Someone crashed through that window, judging by the shards of glass on the lawn outside. And I heard the crash myself," Harrison said. "As soon as the lab boys are ready, I want you two on this." He spun on his heels and left.

Sloan and Perez walked through the Latham mansion slowly. Every guest was gone, with uniformed officers having taken down statements from as many people as they could. The crime lab officers were in the study, dusting for fingerprints and analyzing anything they deemed important. As they walked down another lengthy corridor, Perez shot Sloan a pressing glance.

"I don't buy this at all. First, we're supposed to believe The Wraith exists, and second, that he broke into Latham's mansion—with hundreds of potential witnesses, I might add—to murder Latham's daughter? No way."

"This has mob hit written all over it," Sloan replied. "I agree with you, but I guess with Latham, we have to tread carefully, much as it galls me."

"What is it with you and Latham? I've never understood the hostility you have for him."

"He's crooked, Perez, and let's leave it at that." He exited the house, with Perez close at his heels. "As soon as we get the lab results back, we'll know where to take this."

The two hopped into their unmarked car and gunned it down the drive.

* * * * * *

Grieco paced frantically; Latham remained seated. The two were alone, Latham having excused both Gough and the remaining troupe of his men.

"What do we do? What the hell are we gonna do?" Grieco was losing his cool; this flagrant invasion of the empire's headquarters seemed to unnerve him.

Latham remained silent for a few moments before responding. "Nothing."

Grieco stopped his stride and stared at him in shock. "Am I hearing you right? Nothing? How can we do nothing? Are you crazy? We have to move now! War's been declared. Everything you've done to nail The Wraith has failed. We should've taken decisive action a year ago when I suggested. We must—"

Latham, wild with fury, jerked to his feet and grabbed Grieco by the collar, slamming him against the wall. Grieco, for all his bravado and displays of strength, was a coward deep down, and he knew it.

"You fool!" Latham shrieked. "It wasn't The Wraith. It was *him*!"

Grieco tried to reply, but his breath was being squeezed from him by Latham's powerful grip. "But...but..."

Latham lessened his hold ever so slightly, but didn't let go. "You don't question me. *Ever.* I know who killed my daughter...but there's nothing we can do about *him.* The Wraith doesn't kill, I know him better than anyone. Framing him was all I could think to do."

Latham let Grieco go. The deputy rubbed his throat, chagrined and still on edge. "Him? You mean—"

"The Cobra," Latham said under his breath. He walked back to his seat and sat down, exhausted and feeling dead inside. "Get outta here."

Grieco didn't need to be told twice and hurriedly left the room, leaving Latham alone with his thoughts.

"God help this city," he whispered.

* * * * * *

The morning sun bathed the Sanderson mansion in a gold. The tree-filled grounds glowed in the colors of the fall despite the recent warm weather. Reds, yellows, oranges, purples, all shone brilliantly in the sunlight.

Deep in The Wraith's Lair, Paul, Leena and Max stood in the crime lab, with Paul looking through the microscope.

"Hmm, I thought so," Paul said.

"What is it?" Leena asked.

Paul stood, stretched his back. It had been a long night. Leena yawned.

"Poison. Barbara Latham's lipstick was laced with Xicosin. She was dead in seconds." He rubbed the back of his neck. "The police won't find this out in a hurry with their limited resources. Xicosin is one of the newer synthetic poisons, probably stemming from the Middle East."

"Oh my," Max said.

The secret door above opened with a hum, and Simpson entered with the early morning paper.

"Could this be an enemy of Latham's? A competitor?" Max said.

"Possibly, but why—Yes, Simpson?"

Simpson held up the paper for all to see. "It appears Miss Latham was not the only victim last night."

Paul snatched the paper from Simpson's hands and read the headline then article. "Five die in night of horror! Five people were found dead last night with no explanation. Police are investigating before commenting further. All that was said was that these were no natural deaths." Paul was furious. "This is no enemy of Latham's. This is something else. And with the homeless going missing in recent months..."

Were the homeless abductions and these poisonings linked somehow? If they were, he had nothing to prove it. It was mere speculation, a gut feeling. But something was telling him deep inside that they were linked.

"What's the plan, Chief?" Max asked.

"The lipstick that killed Barbara Latham came from Tavelli Cosmetics. Max, I want you and Leena to go to their Montgomery Street office and see what you can find out. I'll continue examining the lipstick itself. I may be able to discover more. Report to me with your findings, no matter how small."

"Got it," Max said.

Max quickly left the Lair along with Simpson, leaving Leena and Paul along.

"Do you think Tavelli is somehow involved?" Leena asked. "That would be an obvious clue."

"Too obvious. A clue that blatant could be nothing less than—"

"A message!" the two said in unison.

Paul rubbed his chin. "But from whom?"

~ Chapter 18 ~

Tavelli Cosmetics was a smaller cosmetics company than the likes of Revlon, L'Oreal or Maybeline, but no less prestigious. Started a mere fifteen years ago by Charles Tavelli II, his son Charles Tavelli III had taken over when he died four years ago. The elder Tavelli had built the company into an empire from the ground up, specializing in expensive, quality created makeup, fragrances and other cosmetic applications, and while the son hadn't quite the business acumen of his father, the company was nevertheless still healthy. Unlike those other, larger companies, Tavelli was headquartered in the U.S., in Metro City, and not Europe, making the company's products very popular amongst the country's wealthy and elite. Their office on Montgomery Street was modern and vibrant.

The foyer was grand, contemporary and classically designed, with a sweeping part-glass ceiling and ornate, metallic pillars strategically placed. It was mid-morning and foot traffic was hectic, with business people entering and exiting the building.

Leena entered through the spiral doorway, dressed in a long, expensive designer dress, long gloves, bonnet, dark sunglasses and deep crimson lipstick. She wouldn't have looked out of place had she been attending the Kentucky Derby. She strode elegantly toward the front information desk.

"Is Charles in?" she asked the receptionist in a stuffy accent.

"Excuse me?" the receptionist said.

"Charles. Mr. Tavelli to you, of course," she said. "I assume you know the name of the man who employs you?"

The receptionist, a young lady of no more than twenty years old appeared flustered at Leena's insistent and snobby attitude.

"Well, I..." she started.

"Come, come, is he free or not?" Leena was enjoying this.

The receptionist hummed and hawed for a moment.

Leena shot her an icy glance. "You're obviously of no use to me. I shall find Charles on my own. If you see him before I, tell him his lover is waiting for him."

Leena walked past her toward the row of elevators at the rear of the large foyer. Entering the next available elevator, Leena pushed the button for the fifteenth floor—the building's top floor, and the floor she and Max had discovered from an inside source was the location of Charles Tavelli's office.

When she reached the top, she removed her sunglasses and her snobbish persona vanished. She scanned the office doors as she walked past them down the main hall.

"Which one?" she breathed.

Charles Tavelli's office was at the end of the hall. She reached inside her tiny handbag and removed a small compact.

"Let's see if Mr. Tavelli is home."

Leena opened the compact to reveal not makeup and mirror, but intricate wiring and a small receiver. She took the receiver and placed it into her left ear, while holding the open compact toward the door in her right hand. Her eyes widened as Tavelli's voice came through loud and clear through the receiver.

Bless Max's heart for another ingenious device, Leena thought.

"The police were just here," Leena heard Tavelli say. "You said you would cover me, that no one would find out of my involvement. I'm ruined! All those people killed. You promised only Barbara..."

"Hey!" Leena was startled by the cry from a security guard at the end of the hall. The guard looked serious, and the mousy receptionist was right behind him. "Move back from that door, Miss!" the guard yelled.

Leena smiled at them briefly then spun on her heels and ran.

"Stop!" the guard cried.

With the compact still open in her hand, she pressed a small button at its center.

"Get ready," she said into the compact.

She darted quickly into the stairwell, the guard twenty or so feet behind. She could only imagine the look on the guard's face when he reached the roof.

She would be gone.

* * * * * *

On the roof, the guard burst through the door, expecting to corner Leena. He quickly stopped in his tracks, however. She *was* gone. He circled around, not believing that she could have vanished into thin air as she seemingly had. He looked over the edge of the building on all sides. Nothing. The receptionist and Charles Tavelli now joined the guard, Tavelli puffing, struggling to catch his breath.

"Where did she go?" the receptionist asked, totally baffled.

"What the hell's going on here?" Tavelli shrieked, still trying to get his breath back.

The guard looked as puzzled as the rest of them. "I have no idea..." His voice trailed as he headed back to the door, followed by the receptionist. Tavelli, however, stayed on the roof, looking frightened. Sweat began to bead on his brow. He shook with worry as he too finally headed back downstairs.

* * * * * *

Inside the Daimler, Leena leaned back in the leather back seat, picked up the backseat car-phone and dialed. Max looked on in the rear-view mirror, as he geared the car through the city.

"Tavelli's definitely involved, but he's not running the show," she told Paul. "I heard him talking to someone on the phone in his office, but I was nearly caught before I could find out more. I do know that the police have already interviewed him."

"The police are on the right track, but it will no doubt take them awhile to pull what little strings there are together.

You did well. Head back home, darling. The Wraith takes action tonight!"

"Back home, Max," she said, laying the phone back in its cradle.

* * * * * *

Paul paced in his Lair, mulling the situation over in his mind.

What role did Tavelli play in all this? And why? And whom was he working with or for?

So far, he had no answers.

~ Chapter 19 ~

Once night fell on Metro City, shadows seemed to creep along with a life of their own, as if claiming the city in its sinister clutches. In certain parts of the city, lowlifes appeared from their holes, prostitutes took to their street corners, and petty thugs moved to the streets in search of some easy prey.

While the Tavelli Cosmetics building wasn't one of the larger in the city's skyline, it was designed in such a way as to shine light outwards, making it stand out as a pseudo lighthouse; a beacon in the night sky.

The Wraith scaled carefully down the glass and steel wall, lowering himself with a remote controlled line, feeding from a small engine atop the building's roof. Not needing to lower himself very far, The Wraith stopped the mechanism at the fifteenth floor, and deftly opened the window leading into the corridor using a special device of Max's that rendered the alarm receptors in the window useless. Opening the window itself was easy, but it was Max's ingenuity that ensured the safe entrance into the building, overriding the alarm system.

The Wraith dropped silently onto the corridor floor. He tapped at his right temple and infra-red lenses slipped down into place over his eyes. He scanned for beams of light, deadly alarms–lenses located in the walls–but there were none. He crept along the corridor, like the shadowy apparition that was his namesake.

Reaching the mouth of the corridor, The Wraith peered around the corner. A security guard stood by the elevators. He was young and, The Wraith hoped, inexperienced. In an instant, he brought forth a small ball, just slightly larger than a marble, from his belt, and held it aloft briefly, rolling it in his fingers.

He tossed the ball around the corner, along the floor toward the guard. Before the guard could react, the ball came to rest by his feet. Plumes of gas erupted from several small openings. In seconds, the guard was enveloped in thick smoke. The guard managed to grab his radio from his belt and coughed a call for help.

"B-backup needed...help..." The guard's voice trailed off as he fell to the floor unconscious.

When the gas had fully evaporated, The Wraith reached the guard's body. He hadn't anticipated the guard's prompt resourcefulness and had to work in a hurry before reinforcements arrived. He grabbed the guard's radio and examined it closely. It seemed to work only with a specific code keyed in, and the guard had managed to switch it off before he fell.

No calling off the cavalry, he thought. He had to work fast.

Thinking quickly, The Wraith noticed only one of the elevators was operational at this late hour. He pulled a small tube from his belt, similar in size and shape to a tube of toothpaste and, moving over to the elevator, squeezed the tube's contents down the center of the elevator doors. The grey, sticky paste smeared smooth along the length of the join.

"That should hold a while," he said. He did the same along the stairwell's door-frame.

The job done, he made his way over to Tavelli's office, and cautiously entered. The office was bathed in the slight, fluorescent light coming from the small lamp on Tavelli's desk. As with the rest of the building, the office was modern and well furnished, classy and effectual. Behind the desk was a large

leather chair, its back facing the room. As he looked around for anything resembling files, an arm flopped onto the armrest.

"Tavelli!" The Wraith said. "I want answers."

No reply. The Wraith rounded the desk and swiveled the chair around. Charles Tavelli sat there, dead, his throat cut from ear to ear. Despite having seen just about every form of atrocity man could inflict on man, the sight of Tavelli sitting there nevertheless sickened him. A note was stuck to the dead man's tie. The Wraith tore it off in anger. The note read:

BETTER LUCK NEXT TIME!

The Wraith vowed there would be a reckoning—and soon.

~ Chapter 20 ~

It was still night and a northern wind had picked up, bringing the cold of the season back, sweeping through the streets of Gladstone, threatening to extinguish the many open fires struggling to keep the homeless warm. Men, women and children, those unfortunate to live on the streets, bundled up as best as possible with the impending gale, huddling together to keep warm as the fires flickered and fought to stay alight in the worsening conditions.

Inside a dirty and near furniture-less Gladstone apartment, three men sat playing poker, ignoring the noises of the coming maelstrom outside. The walls cracked loudly as they played, but they were too busy with their game to notice.

"C'mon, Ralph. Deal," said Jimmy, the youngest and sleaziest of the trio. His greased hair clashed with his ill-fitting clothes.

The table was scattered with cards, cash, beer bottles, ashtrays and guns.

Ralph, the eldest of the group and the oldest-looking, fidgeted impatiently. "Yeah, yeah," he said. "My luck's gotta change sometime."

As he started to toss the cards out, Riccardo looked up, thinking he'd heard something, something that was not the storm. Riccardo was a renowned snitch and what he didn't know wasn't worth knowing. He was also prone to nervousness. "Hey, you hear that?"

"Hear what?" Ralph asked.

"It's just the storm. Quit stalling and play," Jimmy barked.

Riccardo was somewhat chagrined, and was about to continue with the game when a noise was heard outside the front door. The three whirled to face the door, Jimmy grabbing his gun.

"I definitely heard that!" Ralph said.

They remained still for a long time. Jimmy had his gun cocked, ready and waiting for anything that came for him. Nothing did.

Ralph sniffed as if the sound were nothing after all. "Ah, c'mon, there's no one there. The storm's got us all jumping. We're safe; nobody knows we're here. Let's get back to the game."

No sooner had those words been uttered, a large thud boomed from behind them, careening the door off its hinges, sending timber and plaster in all directions.

The Wraith stood in the doorway, a deep scowl etched into his face.

Both Ralph and Riccardo were thrown from their feet, stunned. Jimmy, still holding his gun, didn't seem able to move.

"Jeez!" he finally said.

Coming back to his senses, Jimmy pointed his piece straight at the oncoming avenger, and pulled the trigger, pumping several shots into The Wraith. In a fast move, The Wraith wrapped his cape around him, appearing in the scant light like a vampiric creature at rest. The bullets bounced harmlessly off the inky cloak.

"Holy!" exclaimed Jimmy. Desperate, he heaved the gun at The Wraith, who easily batted the weapon aside.

Courageous, or perhaps foolheartedly, Jimmy stood his ground and took a pathetic swing at the Dread Avenger, who dodged the attempted blow.

"Damn you!" Jimmy screamed.

The Wraith slammed his fist into Jimmy's stomach, dropping the thug like a stone. Ralph, in the meantime, had snuck around the back of The Wraith. He slammed the butt of his own gun down hard on the hero's skull.

With The Wraith on his knees, Ralph pointed his gun directly at the back of The Wraith's head, smiling in triumph.

"I bet your head ain't bullet-proof," he snickered, ready to make every criminal's dream come true by killing the Dread Avenger of the Underworld. He cocked the pistol slowly, savoring the moment. It was this pause that enabled The Wraith to strike, swiftly and terribly. He swung his arm around, swatting the gun from Ralph's hand. In another instant, he was up and had Ralph's gun arm wrenched behind his back. He slammed Ralph's face into the wall with such force that it caused teeth to crack and loosen.

The Wraith straightened and moved toward Riccardo, who was now pressed against the far wall, shivering.

"Wh-whatya want?" Riccardo managed to say.

"Answers!" snarled The Wraith. He stood before Riccardo, sneering. "You know everything that goes on in this city, Riccardo. The poisonings—Who's responsible?"

Riccardo shook his head. "I...I can't tell you...I can't..."

The Wraith clutched Riccardo's throat with one hand and lifted him off the ground.

"Who is responsible?!" The Wraith roared.

Riccardo fought for breath. The Wraith let go, letting him fall to his feet. Riccardo spluttered and coughed as much air into his lungs as he could.

"Talk!" The Wraith said.

"The...Cobra," Riccardo managed to say. "It's the Cobra." He wanted to take a step back, wanted some breathing room, but he couldn't. The wall was right behind him. "All I know is this city's in trouble, deep trouble. You wanna know anythin' else, ask Robert Latham."

He ran past The Wraith, escaping through the destroyed doorway.

* * * * * *

That name slammed into The Wraith like a jackhammer. *Could it be...him?* He stood there, pondering that question. Was Latham somehow involved in the poisonings? Was he involved in his own daughter's death? He doubted it. Latham was a monster, that much was true, but when it came to his own family, the crime lord was as loving and protective as any husband and father. The matter that burned in his mind was the Cobra. Could it really be him? After all these years? Was Riccardo right, was the Cobra responsible for the rash of poisonings? Was he also behind the mysterious Magnus Khan, behind the senseless slaughter and kidnapping of countless homeless men? If Latham had the answers, The Wraith would soon find out what they were—and fast.

* * * * * *

Robert Latham strode briskly to his car in the underground garage of the Latham Industries building. The garage was virtually empty this late hour. He was working late again, as he had been since his daughter's death, pouring himself into his work like never before. Briefcase in hand, he reached his Mercedes and remotely switched the alarm off with an audible beep. As he reached for the door handle, he heard a slight noise behind him. He turned.

"Oh, it's you," he said nonchalantly, as if expecting a late night visit.

The Wraith stood close, forcing Latham to press back against his car. "What do you know of the Cobra?" he asked with a grunt, trying to intimidate Latham, who usually didn't intimidate quite so easily.

"I have absolutely no idea what you're talking about," Latham said with a huff. Latham reached for his car door, but The Wraith blocked his path.

"You're lying! Somehow, you're involved in all these deaths, including your own daughter's! And you didn't hesitate attempting to frame me for her murder."

Latham turned and stared into The Wraith's eyes, anger burning in his face, as though he were to immediately and irrevocably lose control...but he soon recovered, and even smiled. He leaned close, still smiling. "I will tell you this, superhero—the Cobra will deal with you the way you and I swat a fly. You're nothing to him, less than nothing." Latham raised an eyebrow, seemingly confident and assured of that.

"May I go now? It's late and I still have my daughter's funeral to prepare."

Without waiting for a response, Latham got into his car and sped off, leaving The Wraith in a gust of smoke.

~ Chapter 21 ~

Detective Bob Sloan sat at his desk the next morning, deep in thought. He hated when a case came up that seemed unsolvable. The thought he was being too hard on himself did occur to him. The poisonings had only recently transpired, but he had a burning feeling in his gut that he wasn't going to be happy with the outcome of this case. As he pondered this, thoughts of the Michael Reeve case came flooding back to him, as did the more recent homeless case. The failures of those, particularly the Reeve case—his friend— hit him hard. Sloan hated how the corruption-filled police force had treated one of their own.

It was early and the morning shift staff had yet to fully filter in. Rosa Perez arrived and eyed Sloan curiously.

"Morning," Sloan said halfheartedly. She stopped by his desk. He squinted at her, trying to work out if she looked different. "You done something to your hair?"

She frowned. She wasn't wearing any makeup, as authorities had advised of the public with the recent tainting of certain cosmetic products. It had become evident in the last few days that more than just Tavelli products were tainted. "Bob, how long you been here?"

Sloan wiped his eyes, but he couldn't hide the fact he had been there all night–again.

"Not another all-nighter?" she moaned.

Sloan ignored her, not caring whether she disapproved or not. If he could withstand his wife's protests, he could certainly stand to hear hers.

"Just been thinking," he said. After a moment, he stood and pulled the jacket from the back of his chair. "Over twenty dead now, Perez. Twenty! And we still haven't even identified the poison. We will though." He rubbed his tired face with consternation. "Like we needed this on top of the missing person's case we've hit the wall with. All those homeless men... You know yourself how many people have been murdered, but how many have vanished throughout the country over the last year, let alone Metro City? They've just vanished off the face of the Earth."

"I lost count after the first few hundred," Perez admitted.

Sloan struggled into his jacket, and went past her.

"Where are we headed?" she asked.

"Morgue. I want answers. Now."

* * * * * *

The Metro City morgue was a busy place at any hour. Murder wasn't a rare occurrence in the city and the staff there were kept constantly on their toes. New corpses arrived at a reasonably regular rate on the best of days and, despite it being early in the morning, today was no exception. Sloan and Perez were in the morgue's main examination room, watching as Chief Medical Examiner Howard Boynce covered up the latest cadaver.

"Tell me something, Howard. I need something," Sloan said.

Boynce, a tall and thin man with penetrating eyes behind thin glasses and a bouffant hairstyle, stared at the two police officers. He removed his gloves. "What can I say? I'm waiting to hear from head lab. With the meager resources here at our disposal, we have no way of determining the identity of the poison used without outside assistance."

"All we know so far then, is that it's being used in women's cosmetics across all brands and types. Store recalls can only move so fast," Perez said.

"Correct," Boynce said. "We're looking at, potentially, more casualties here, I'm afraid. At least for the next few days."

Sloan, frustrated as hell, threw Boynce an angry look. "Dammit, Howard, don't you have any clues, here?"

Boynce was unfazed. "Sure, I could give you a guess, but that wouldn't do us any good. I can't tell you how many poisons and toxins there are in existence that we cannot detect at this 'marvelous' facility. As frustrating as it is, we simply have to wait for the results to come back to us from head lab."

"More than twenty people have been murdered! I can't wait any longer while some wacko killer out there kills again and again. I have to do something, dammit!" Sloan stormed off.

Perez tried her best to stop him. "Wait! We can't go half-cocked like this without all the facts."

"And I'm not gonna sit back and wait 'til God knows when to get some test results back. And I'm sure as hell not gonna lose another case the way I did the Reeve one."

"Bob…"

"C'mon, we're wasting time here. I'm hitting the streets. If you wanna join me, then let's go."

Leaving Boynce behind, the two officers exited the examining room and out toward a pretty long-haired receptionist, a nameplate with the name Natalie Black atop her desk front and center. As they passed her, she carefully picked up the phone, and began dialing as the two officers left.

* * * * * *

She tapped her fingers on her desk impatiently as she waited for her call to be answered. Finally, "Master," she murmured quietly under her breath, "the police have been here. They know nothing. They are running around like lost children." She paused. "I am yours to command." She hung up, and grinned.

* * * * * *

In one of Metro City's innumerable deserted warehouses, deep within the squalid recesses of the dockside landscape, a pagoda–an almost pyramid-style structure with glistening smooth walls sloping up to a point—sat at its center, lighting up its lifeless surroundings. Inside the unique structure-within-a-structure, a costumed monster of a man sat on an intricately designed throne, grand and intimidating. The Cobra.

The Cobra stood, stalking forth from the shadows from which he sat. He was huge, almost seven feet tall, and as broad as an ox, with a menacing, cobra-shaped scar over his right eye, milky white of color. He wore a dark red, scaly suit, running smooth against his muscled body.

He turned and faced a mass of men a few hundred strong, all standing at attention, staring back at him silently, their expressions blank.

"Are you ready, my foot soldiers?" the Cobra thundered. "Are you ready to take what is mine?"

"Yes, Master!" the crowd shouted in perfect harmony.

"Good," said the Cobra. "But I must soften this city further. First, I spread death. Then I spread fear. Now, I will destroy!" He smirked ever so slightly. "Then, the city will be yours to take in my name." The Cobra moved back toward his throne. "And The Wraith will be mine." He clenched his fist as though clutching the city in his hand, crushing it, with his army there before him, watching—waiting—to destroy in his name.

The hour was soon at hand...

~ Chapter 22 ~

Brooding alone in his antique chair, Paul sat silently in the library. He often sat like this, allowing the darkness to wash over him and his thoughts. While only mid-afternoon, all the blinds were drawn, giving the *feel* of night. He was comfortable here, sometimes more so than anywhere else. His mind was filled with the turmoil that was now raging through the city. Men murdered, many having vanished, possibly kidnapped, in their hundreds if not thousands; innocents being slaughtered by some maniac poisoner, and now the Cobra. Questions tumbled over and over in his brain. *Is the Cobra responsible for all these atrocities? What does he want after all these years? Could it still be revenge?*

Max entered. "Chief?" His voice was soft.

"Hmm?"

"You wanted me to let you know when the new gym equipment was ready."

"Hmm?" Paul repeated. Max stood before him. He snapped out of it. "Oh, yes, thank you, Max."

Paul moved to stand, but stopped when his watch vibrated. He looked down at his arm, saw the flashing Omega logo on his Seamaster watch, then looked at Max intently. They knew what that meant.

Max removed a remote control device from his pocket before Paul had a chance to, and pressed the button. Once again, with a whirring of gears, the secret door slid open, and Paul swiftly entered, making his way into the heart of the Lair. He placed a pair of headphones over his head; Max arrived by his side.

"Report," said Paul into the microphone. He listened intently. "Thank you. Out."

Paul removed the headphones, but said nothing, lost in thought.

"Something?" Max asked.

"One of my most trusted snitches. Something big's going down tonight, possibly at key locations throughout the city. That was all he could say." Paul swiveled in his chair, facing Max. "It's the Cobra, I know it. He's out for revenge. Revenge against me, against everything I hold dear." He paused. "Whatever he's planning is happening tonight. We've got to stop him." He stood and began to pace. "We'll be stretched thin."

"We have to warn the police, make them aware," Max said.

"Warn them of what? We have no proof, absolutely nothing they'd believe. I know the police force, the amount of prank calls they receive, there's no way they'll take any anonymous call like this seriously."

"Then what do we do?"

"Whatever we can," he said. "Equipment and costumes ready?"

"As always."

He stopped pacing. "I'll alert Leena, while you check the equipment once more."

Max rolled his eyes, but complied. "Sure, okay." He retreated toward the costumes.

Paul sat back down and contacted Leena. "Leena, come in darling."

Max checked each costume in turn, giving each his approval. He then moved over to a small table nearby and checked every small piece of equipment that Paul utilized as The Wraith. Re-breather, smoke and knockout gas capsules, rope, grapples, weapons. All seemed to be in perfect working order. He returned to Paul's side.

"We're prepared as much as we can be," Paul said. "Now we just wait and hope we learn more before tonight."

* * * * * *

Exiting the Metro City Police headquarters building, Sloan and Perez strolled to their unmarked. Sloan was as determined as ever, perhaps more so, while Perez, as was usually the case, stood stoically by his side.

"Where are we headed now?" she asked.

"Back to Tavelli Cosmetics. Tavelli's dead. You can't tell me that's a coincidence. He knew something; maybe was even involved somehow."

"We don't have any proof of that, Bob. But you're right, something's not kosher there. Think we can get anyone to talk?"

"If anyone there knows something, which isn't guaranteed, we'll make them talk. After Tavelli, we hit the streets—informants, hookers, pimps, bully boys, bouncers—we talk to them all."

Perez sighed. Sloan, despite his determination, was tired at the sound of yet another all-nighter. There had been far too many of those as of late, but he knew it couldn't be helped. The city was nearly a war zone right now. They had to keep things as much under control as possible. As bad as the situation was, Sloan knew it could easily be worse.

The two detectives worked hard, interviewing dozens of Tavelli staff members, as well as the aforementioned street people. Some were eager to talk, though they were the ones with nothing really to say. Most, however, were wary, even scared. A small handful were even so scared as to try and fight to get away from them, terrified of possibly revealing too much, and what that may entail. Over the course of the afternoon, the two detectives talked to at least three dozen men and women. None of them knew a thing or, as Sloan and Perez suspected, weren't willing to reveal anything.

It was now four hours later and night had fallen. Now on the far side of town, they made their way back to their car, exhausted and irritated.

"Everyone's scared. Somebody's putting the fear into them, Bob. They're not just scared about the poisonings, they fear the one responsible," Perez said.

"They're scared enough to stay silent, that's for sure. Did you notice a few of them started to say something then stopped? You're right. Some either suspect, or even know, who's responsible. Dammit, they're more afraid of *them* than they are of *us*."

Sloan flopped into the driver's seat; Perez took her seat beside him.

"The thing that scares me is I got the impression we're in for more," Sloan said.

Perez looked at him with concern. "More poisonings?"

"Maybe or maybe something else. I don't know." Sloan exhaled audibly.

"We heading back to base?"

"Yeah, we can write our reports while we think of where else to take this tonight. I'm not giving up."

Sloan started the car and sped into the busy city traffic, their horns blaring at him.

* * * * * *

Within his antechamber, the Cobra peered at his lieutenant, Magnus Khan. Long-haired and bearded, Khan looked for all the world like an ancient Mongolian warlord. He stood proudly alongside his master.

"Are the explosives set?" asked the Cobra.

"Almost complete at last report, my Master, at the locations you specified."

The Cobra sauntered over to a small, exotic table at the far end of the room. He picked up an intricate piece of explosive equipment. "Good," he said. "Step two is now almost complete." He placed it back down on the table and spun on his heels, walking back toward Khan. "The Wraith will attempt to stop us tonight, naturally. He will fail. But know this: for this city to be completely mine, there must be a reckoning between us." The Cobra's voice deepened and hardened at the mere mention of The Wraith.

Khan remained absolutely still and silent, whether he knew of the history between the two or not.

The Cobra continued. "The Wraith will die, as I have long promised, and as I fulfill my vow to this...Latham. And then Metro City will be mine, as I fulfill my destiny."

Khan bowed with a graceful poise not expected from one so bulky and muscular. "Your soldiers await your further commands, my Master."

"Prepare them. The city awaits us."

~ Chapter 23 ~

The Daimler cut through the city traffic. Max was at the wheel as usual, while Paul and Leena sat in the spacious rear, discussing the night's possibilities.

"Do we know what we're up against?" Leena asked, squirming slightly in the leather seat.

"The Cobra is planning something big. That's all we were able to ascertain this afternoon. Just what and how, we don't know," Paul said.

Leena looked at him intently. "You act as though you know him."

He pulled the center section of the backseat down, revealing a compact costume and equipment compartment. "I do. That's why I'm so afraid. I know what he's capable of." He removed the neatly folded costume from its base, separating the cowl from the rest of the uniform. "My history with him is a long story. Perhaps one day I'll fill you in on it."

Leena appeared nonplussed.

"We'll spread out, cover as much of the city as possible. Keep an eye out for anything unusual or suspicious." Paul began to loosen his tie. "Keep in constant touch especially if you spot anything."

Max veered the car into a side alley and steered it into a secluded spot, parking quickly. He, Leena and The Wraith stepped forth from the car.

"Max, cover the north side," The Wraith said. "Leena, the eastern section we outlined earlier. I'll cover the south and west, with the help of a few of my contacts. A few more should be in your areas as well, so keep your eye out."

Max nodded and headed away quickly. The Wraith held Leena close.

"Are you ready?" he asked, not in The Wraith's fearsome voice, but in Paul's more gentle, yet still deep, tone.

"For anything," she replied. While she had been fully and expertly trained for any eventuality, The Wraith knew she still feared for the safety of the city tonight. And with good reason. "Come back to me safe, darling."

They kissed.

* * * * * *

Later, The Wraith was atop one of the city's tallest buildings, the aptly named Metro Towers. He had his infra-red mini-binoculars out, scanning the city for any signs of anything out of the ordinary. There were none.

"What are we looking for?" The Wraith asked himself. "What can the Cobra be planning?"

The Wraith dropped down the building's fire escape, and ran down the back alley, trying to cover as much ground as possible, his cape billowing out behind him. The Wraith sprinted a few blocks then climbed the highest building closest to him, and again watched vigilantly. He repeated the move several times, seeing nothing with each climb, before arriving at a building across from Latham Industries.

Perched there, he finally saw what he had been searching for. Atop the Latham building were four men, dressed vaguely like ninjas, moving about on the roof.

Not security guards, The Wraith thought, studying them closely before moving again.

The "ninjas" were placing large sets of explosives in each corner of the building. Working almost robotically, they turned at the sound of crunching gravel.

"Men of the Cobra!" roared The Wraith.

Without delay, the four ninja-clad men launched themselves at The Wraith, attempting to overpower him. While it was four-on-one, it was clearly a mismatch—in The Wraith's favor. While they were strong and clearly brave, they lacked skill and co-ordination, and it was easy for The Wraith to dodge their blows and launch his own offensive maneuvers. Smashing the skulls of two of them together, The Wraith slammed a powerful right into the jaw of a third, leaving three of them incapacitated. The remaining "ninjas" foolishly fought on, but it was quickly over.

The Wraith ripped the thug's mask off. "Answers. Now!"

The man said nothing, appearing drugged or mesmerized somehow, yet strangely no less alert. The Eyes of Judgment on The Wraith's chest began to glow a ghostly yellow as he held the thug in his thrall.

"Where is the Cobra? What is he planning?"

"I can't tell you," the man said. "I will not betray my master."

Half expecting this, The Wraith forced the hapless man to stare straight into the Eyes of Judgment, turning the Judgment Stare on him with full force.

"Confess!" The Wraith said.

The man, evidently in pain, but almost impossibly appearing to be fighting it, stuttered, "No...I...I cannot..." And he cried out in anguish, his body falling limp in The Wraith's arms. The Wraith dropped him, letting him fall to the gravel.

The man curled up in the foetal position and began to babble incoherently. Or was he? The Wraith had never seen such a reaction from someone who had experienced the Judgment Stare before.

"Wasntmyfaultnotmedidntdoitnotmyfaultmademedoit... " the man rambled.

The Wraith grabbed him by the collar, jerking him up and clear off the ground.

"Answer me!" he spat in the thug's face.

"Explosionsthroughoutcitylathampolicetavellitownsquares oldierstoinvade...notmyfaultmademedoit... "

"Explosions? When? Tonight?"

Weakening, the man barely uttered: "N...n...now..." And he died, the struggle between whatever was controlling him and The Wraith's induced guilt seemingly too powerful to bear.

The Wraith looked around and noticed the large objects in each corner of the roof. "Explosives?" He realized the truth. "Lord!" The Wraith's jaw dropped, and in the seconds he had left, he heard at least two explosions rip through the night before the Latham Industries roof detonated in four incredible balls of flame, swallowing him in a world of heat.

~ Chapter 24 ~

Just as the explosions detonated, releasing their destructive energy fourfold, The Wraith leaped to safety. The incredible force of the fiery inferno carried him toward the rooftop of the adjacent building. He landed hard, his costume damaged, burning debris raining down around him. Thinking quickly as no other man could, he was up on his feet and dropped over the edge of this building, landing instinctively on that building's fire escape, knowing full well it was there. No one knew the city like the Dread Avenger of the Underworld.

Now able to catch his breath slightly, The Wraith spotted from this vantage point two other explosions in the city, though he wasn't quite sure of their exact locations. Despite being bruised and battered, he was relatively unharmed, his lightning fast reflexes had served him well once again. Realizing he needed to quickly get his bearings, he hurried down the fire escape and onto the street. Now a safe distance back from the carnage, he was able to see the horrendous damage.

"Lord," he said quietly. The top ten or so floors of the Latham Industries building were destroyed; the surrounding buildings were also partially in flames. Rage welled up inside him, fury over what was being done to his city. He vowed once again that the person responsible, the Cobra, would pay dearly for this.

Max and Leena came in on the radio. The Wraith held a hand to his ear as their fervent cries rang out.

"Chief, I heard an explosion, possibly more than one. Are you okay?" said Max.

"Darling? What's happened, are you all right?" came Leena's voice.

"I'm fine, both of you. One at a time," The Wraith said.

"An explosion just detonated, though none close to me. I'm sure I heard at least two," Max said.

"I'm closer to one of the explosions though I can't make out what was hit," Leena said.

"Stay put," The Wraith said. "Emergency personnel are undoubtedly on their way and I suspect we'll be needed elsewhere." The Wraith paused for a moment. "Stand by."

The Wraith switched his radio off and stared up at the devastation of his surroundings. *What could he and his small team do now?* The thought buzzed in his brain as he struggled for an answer.

* * * * * *

The Metro City Police headquarters was one of the buildings hit by the Cobra's fury. Sloan and Perez had just arrived at the scene mere minutes after the explosion, and the sight horrified them. Through the plumes of smoke and dust, they could see the building was gone, rubble and flame all that was left of the once proud bastion of justice. The bodies and body parts strewn about twisted their stomachs. Perez bolted from the car and bent over and heaved, unable to control herself.

"No..." Sloan finally managed to utter. He helped Perez to her feet. She wiped her mouth, tears in her eyes. "We gotta check for survivors."

Frantically looking about, Perez spotted movement from one side of the rubble. "Over there."

One officer was stumbling toward them. Sloan and Perez raced to his side and helped him back a safe distance away and sat him down. Sloan ran back to the carnage, with Perez quickly joining him. There were a few officers moving—some crawling, some on their knees, some prone but breathing. In turn, Sloan and Perez were able to move all of them away from the flames. All in all, there were eleven officers they were able to find and help. Blackened by the dirt and soot, Sloan looked like a war veteran who had just come back from the battlefield.

"There's gotta be more," he said. He was about to move back into the firestorm when Commissioner Harrison's car screeched to a halt beside theirs. He was at their side quicker than a man of his age and size was expected to.

"I was coming back from dinner with the Mayor when I heard the explosions," he wheezed.

Sloan looked at him incredulously. "Explosions?"

"At least two or three; I can't be sure."

Perez dropped her head into her hands; it was open warfare. Sloan looked stunned, even his years-long experience in a city as filled with inequity and vice as Metro City couldn't have prepared him for this, she knew.

Ambulance, fire and rescue personnel arrived at the scene, and Harrison retreated to meet and confer with their commanding officers. Perez went over to the survivors. As paramedics surrounded her, helping the injured, Perez knelt beside a colleague, a friend of hers, and tried to comfort him as best she could. He was horribly burned, his flesh boiled and bloody.

"It's okay, Fred, you're going to be okay," she said, trying to reassure herself as much as she was him. Fred opened his eyes slightly but his eyes were too swollen for him to see properly. He tried to speak, but no words came. He passed away quietly in Perez's arms. She wept, unable to keep her strength up any longer. Sloan stood by her for a moment, but soon left her alone to grieve.

He came back to her after a time. "Jeez, Perez," Sloan said, "there's not many of us left. What are we dealing with here? Terrorists?"

Perez tried to gather herself together as the paramedics began taking away the injured and dead. "Has to be," she said. "Who else could organize something this large a scale?"

She was a wreck and she knew it. Tears still streamed down her face. "Dammit! We have to do something! It's like nine-eleven all over again."

Harrison returned to them; the emergency crews worked feverishly in the background. Fire crews trained their hoses on the powerful flames blazing through the ruins of the police building. The flames were too intense for rescue crews to continue the search for survivors, and they waited nervously but intensely behind the front line of the fire teams.

"As best we can tell," Harrison said, "there have been three or four explosions. I'm told Latham Industries was one, Town Square another. Emergency personnel are stretched to the limit. This is all we're getting for the time being."

"What do we do now?" Sloan asked.

"I'm calling in the National Guard, as well as all off-duty officers, as few as they may be. We need every person available right now. If need be, I'll call in all city staff—garbage collectors, librarians, whatever it takes." Harrison was clearly fatigued but his iron will still shone through.

Harrison moved over to his car and began to bark orders into his radio. Perez slumped to the ground, trying to regain some of her strength. As she took long, strained breaths, she craned her head upwards suddenly. She raised her eyebrow.

"Bob, you hear that?"

"Hear what?"

They didn't have to wait long to find out. Far down the street, they could make out a mass of people coming toward them, marching as though an invading force. Perez stood, and with Sloan and the returned Harrison, tried to make out what was going on. As the crowd marched steadily closer, like some mad horde, they wondered what nightmare had brought forth this army from hell.

~ Chapter 25 ~

The Wraith frantically leapt from rooftop to rooftop, trying to get to the location of another rescue site, or to find and alert the authorities. There was nothing he could do at Latham Industries; the obliteration was too complete for any one man to fight. The city's police headquarters was nearest to him, and he guessed rescue personnel would congregate there. He needed to alert them to the full dangers they would soon face—that of the Cobra. The Wraith stopped abruptly and looked down into the street. Beneath him were an army of men, hundreds at least, all marching in unison toward the police at the end of the street. The Cobra had made another deadly move.

The kidnapped homeless, The Wraith suddenly thought. Everything became clear to him then.

"Chief!" came Max's voice from the radio. "Bands of men are marching down Queen Street. Looks like hundreds of them, all headed into the city. Leena's with me now."

"They're here too," The Wraith said, "heading toward what's left of the police force."

"You mean—"

"Do the best you can," he said. "I've got to do whatever *I* can here." The Wraith signed off.

Moving over to the other side of the building, he dropped over the edge, using his cape to glide safely to street level. He had to do something. He would not let this city fall without a fight. He would struggle until his last breath. He clenched his jaw, turned and ran in the direction of police headquarters.

* * * * * *

Standing on the rooftop of a small building, Max re-attached his radio to his belt. Leena was concerned as she stood alongside him. Max turned to face her, his features drawn in grave unease.

"They're marching toward police headquarters as well. Throughout the entire city for all we know," Max said.

"What can we do?" she asked.

"All we can."

Leena nodded in agreement. Looking down into the street, she knew the job was enormous, but she also knew that Paul would never give up. Neither would she. Looking at the swarming masses, Leena noticed an elderly man shuffle into the street ahead of the army of men.

"That old man," she cried.

"We have to get down there!" Max exclaimed.

Down on street level, the old man waved a starter horn in front of him as if he were holding a gun. He was limping, walking with a cane, and perhaps not totally mentally competent, but he appeared a tough old bird, and while he was roughly in his eighties, he still had a way about him that bespoke of the military.

"Get outta my city," the old man yelled.

The army of men marched forward, his words meaning nothing.

"Get outta here," he yelled again.

The old man started to limp forward, as though to meet the oncoming army, but was stopped by Max and Leena screeching to a halt in front of him in a beaten up old car.

"Get him in the car!" Max said.

Leena got out and bundled the man into the car and joined him in the backseat. The army was almost upon them.

Max revved the car's engine. "Hang on."

With as much power as the old car could muster, Max aimed it straight at the oncoming army. Max kept his foot on the peddle, but the men refused to halt or to move to the side.

Despite being in league with their mortal enemy, despite the Cobra being responsible for untold deaths and horror, The Wraith had sworn never to take a life, no matter what the circumstance, and those who fought by his side, those who took on his lifelong mission as their own, had to abide by the same. Knowing this, Max swerved the car violently to the right, smashing into a parked car.

The army was upon them. Several of them bashed the car with fists and sticks, some climbing onto the car, ready to murder those inside.

"Max!" Leena shrieked.

One of the swarm smashed the window nearest her and reached through, attempting to yank her through the opening. The madman managed to grab a hold of her hair. She struggled as best she could in the cramped backseat. The old man alongside her reached out with his starter horn and sounded it into the attacker's face.

"Take that!" the old man said.

The attacker staggered back, seemingly disoriented and appeared as though he wasn't aware of his actions or his location. Leena saw Max notice this instantly.

"Look," he said. "Loud noise affects them. They must be brainwashed somehow. It's as if loud noise breaks or interferes with whatever's controlling them."

Max blared the car horn, trying to affect as many of the men as possible. The old man continued to sound his starter horn, reveling in the success of this new strategy. The men around the car reeled back, dazed and confused.

"Leena, quickly, while they're stunned, get out and into another car," Max said. "If we both drive through these guys with our horns blaring, I think we might be able to break through whatever's controlling them."

Without hesitation, Leena got out and dashed through the men. Bumping into several of them, Leena arrived at the car nearest her and smashed her elbow through the driver's side window. Hopping in, she hot-wired it speedily (one of the many skills she learned to gain the honor of fighting by her lover's side). She inched the car out into the street and pressed down hard on the steering wheel's horn. Max continued doing the same, and moved out slowly to join her driving through the large group of men, all of whom staggered back, some clutching their heads, others falling to the ground, writhing as they fought the incredible control which held them in its thrall.

She could see Max mouth the words, "It's working."

The men began to drop to the ground, passing out, the continued onslaught of noise ultimately proving successful in breaking the hold of the Cobra.

"We have to spread the word," he yelled across to Leena. She nodded in agreement.

Their work done, Max got out of his car and moved over to examine the bodies littering the street. He checked for a pulse on one of them. The man by his feet was alive. Next, he forced open the eyes of several of them. Leena did the same. All were glazed over and non-responsive. The old man gloated over the bodies as if he defeated them all single-handedly.

"They're okay; all alive, though weakened. But whatever was controlling them appears to have lost its effectiveness. Loud noise definitely freed them," Max said as he continued examining a few of the unconscious men. "But I can't say what state these men will be in when they awaken." He straightened and scratched his head. "We have to let the Chief know. If he can get enough people together maybe these zombies can be beaten."

Leena glanced around and knew this battle was won. But the war...the war would go on. One they had to win or all would be lost.

* * * * * *

Inside his hidden command center, the Cobra paced before the last two dozen of his men, the last of his stolen army. These were the remainder of the kidnapped.

"You will carry out my orders to the letter and to the last man," the Cobra said. "You will die gladly in my name, should I so wish it." The Cobra's right, marled eye glowed with supernatural force, a power that enabled him to beguile anyone he chose. This was the power of the Cobra. Through this ability, through his own incredible force of will, he was able to enthrall men to do his bidding, to do anything he wanted. Whether it was in their nature or not was irrelevant. "Swear it!" he finished.

"Yes, Master!" the men said together.

Magnus Khan appeared by his side, stoic and tall.

"These are the last," the Cobra said. "Set them forth."

"Yes, my Master," Khan replied.

Entering his antechamber, the Cobra turned to face Khan, entering behind him. "I bring death and destruction upon Metro City. I hold its fate in the palm of my hand." He closed his hand into a fist. "Once my soldiers have carried out my orders, I will collect my share of pain. And then it will be down to the two of us, The Wraith and myself, battling for the ultimate prize, as it was meant to be." The Cobra sat. "Now, let loose the final horde. Alert me when it is time."

"Yes, my Master," Khan replied, retreating from the antechamber to do his bidding.

~ Chapter 26 ~

The battle on George Street escalated when the army of men attacked what was left of the police force and the emergency personnel. The Wraith watched, preparing to enter the fray at just the right moment. He could see Sloan, his firearm exhausted, fighting like a man possessed, punching, kicking and dealing with every man that came his way.

"Jeez, they're everywhere!" Sloan yelled above the noise of combat.

As they struggled valiantly against all odds, The Wraith could see that, despite their courage, they would soon be overwhelmed by the horde. They pressed on.

At this point, a thick cloud of smoke erupted from the center of the battle, engulfing everyone.

"What the—?" Sloan spluttered.

"Tear gas?" the Commissioner questioned. He sniffed the air. "No, it's not." Through the screen of gas, a dark shape appeared, moving swiftly, fighting.

Harrison bellowed an order. "Get in there while they're distracted. Push forward!"

The smoke began to clear.

The police fought with new-found energy, and with the help of this new ally, were finally beginning to make headway. Sloan was the first to see their ally was The Wraith!

"Holy...it's him!" was all he managed to say.

"Stand fast," The Wraith said.

Before anyone else could speak up, Perez pointed out more men turning in to the street a block away. The new army was approaching at a rapid pace.

"Oh no," she said.

The Wraith took the initiative and rushed into the fray of battle with a cry akin to that of ancient tribal warriors. Fighting ferociously, The Wraith used every method of hand-to-hand combat he knew of to deal with this army of evil. The Wraith was soon joined by the police and emergency services, Harrison leading them, holding an old post aloft.

"Keep fighting, don't hold back!" the Commissioner cried.

They fought ferociously in all-out urban warfare—punching, kicking, even biting—whatever it took, with whatever weapons they could lay their hands on, the forces for good fought side-by-side. It was intense, with the brainwashed drones having strength of numbers on their side, but they were undisciplined, unfocused, unskilled. It was because of this that The Wraith and the others began to gain the advantage, and pressed forward.

The Wraith had just laid a massive right to one of the attackers when his radio began to beep an incoming call.

"Chief!" came Max's harried voice.

"Quickly, I haven't time," The Wraith said.

"We've figured out how to stop them," he said. "Loud noise. We've been using car horns. Somehow it disrupts their equilibrium, disorients them, weakens the Cobra's control over them. He's brainwashed them somehow."

"Understood." And The Wraith broke contact. He made a break for the nearest car. "Quickly! Noise affects them!"

He smashed his way into the parked car and started the engine, blaring the horn as quickly as he could. The attackers closest to the car stopped. The noise distressed them as Max had promised.

"Drive through them! Get to as many as possible!" Harrison yelled as they all made their way to an empty car to join The Wraith. With The Wraith at the head of the strange procession, the cars inched through the attackers, all horns blaring, reaching as many of the army as possible.

Arriving at the end of the mass of men, The Wraith jumped from his car. "Keep going. I need you all to keep them distracted."

With the zombies now reeling, The Wraith made quick work of them, fighting his way through the crowd, knocking each out in turn. Sloan joined him, clearly wanting to be in the thick of the action. The Wraith and Sloan fought back-to-back—The Wraith as skilled and exact as always; Sloan, less skilled in hand-to-hand combat, but showing a strength and grit he was well renowned for. With the last few remaining attackers, the rest of the police and emergency services joined them to mop up the rest.

Sloan slammed his fist into the very last of them, before cocking his head toward The Wraith. "We're gonna have words after this," he said.

Ignoring this, something else caught The Wraith's eye. Though no one else seemed to notice, the Cobra appeared from the shadows and beckoned him from a nearby balcony. Harrison and the rest of the men stood amongst the many bodies, taking stock, with the still-burning wreckage of the destroyed police headquarters raging behind them.

* * * * * *

The Wraith stood in the deep pit of a long abandoned building site. Poised on the balls of his feet, he finally faced the mastermind behind the war on Metro City and its citizens. The Cobra stood across from him a distance back, his large frame bristling with power.

"Cobra," The Wraith said. "Abdelkrim."

"You are not the man I knew," the Cobra began, "and yet you are he. Intriguing." He smiled. "Regardless, destiny has finally brought us together."

The Wraith scowled but remained still.

The Cobra continued. "Now let us see who is truly worthy of being master of this city."

~ Chapter 27 ~

Max and Leena arrived at police headquarters exhausted, but none the worse for wear for their incredible ordeal. They stayed back from the view of the officials there, watching intently, but saw no sign of The Wraith.

"They seem to have won the battle here. Where's Paul?" Leena whispered.

"I don't know, but we obviously got the information to him in time judging by what we can see here," Max said.

"What do we do?"

"We find the Chief."

They retreated back from the wreckage and disappeared from view.

* * * * * *

The group outside police headquarters was resting; Harrison in particular was breathing heavily. He sat motionless in the front seat of his car, mopping his brow, trying to regain his composure as best he could. Sloan paced back and forth in front of the car, while Perez sat on the ground close by.

"Dammit, we had him and we let him get away!" Sloan said. "He could have given us so many answers."

"Bob, calm down," Perez said seemingly annoyed. "There'll be other chances. He's revealed himself now."

"You don't believe—"

"Quiet down," Harrison said. "If you're thinking that The Wraith is behind all this, you're mistaken."

Sloan eyed his boss intently. "Tonight could have just been a show, to divert attention away from himself, to make us think he's not responsible." Maybe he was clutching at straws, he thought, but he was just so angry that they had fallen victim to a lunatic out of the funny books.

Harrison sighed. "Think, Sloan. Wouldn't it have been much easier had he not revealed himself at all? The Wraith is not responsible for tonight's disaster."

Sloan stopped pacing when he realized the truth. "You know The Wraith, don't you? You've known he existed all this time. My God, I can see it." He paused briefly. "And you said nothing? I can't believe this!"

Harrison, a stern look on his face, stood. "I don't know The Wraith. I don't know who he is, and I know nothing whatsoever about him. I have long suspected he wasn't the bogeyman we've heard about or the myth this city has built him up to be. I wasn't surprised to see him appear tonight when we needed him, and I *know* he's here to help, nothing more."

Sloan moved to say more, but stopped himself, realizing finally with whom he was talking to. He ran his fingers through his hair.

"So what do we do now?" Perez asked. The question wasn't directed at anyone in particular.

"We wait for the National Guard to arrive. We continue doing what we can here until further help arrives," Harrison said.

"And what about The Wraith?" Sloan queried.

"On that score, we do nothing...for now."

* * * * * *

Robert Latham stared, fuming, at the remains of the headquarters of his international conglomerate. Years of work —legitimate or otherwise—building his empire. Was destroying it worth it?

And it was an empire, Latham thought, one which he wanted to rival any in history. Latham was nothing if not egocentric. But he also had the money and the power to back up his ambitions. And no matter what he'd been through recently, no matter that he, in reality, had sacrificed his own headquarters, even his own daughter, in his mad quest for power and vengeance, he knew deep inside he wouldn't let any of it stop him. Nay, he would go on. He would rise stronger than ever before, and he would prevail. Not the police, not rival cartels or ambitious underlings—not even The Wraith will be able to stand in his way, let alone stop him—not completely. Despite the dreadful sight before him, Latham couldn't help but smile, for he reckoned this to be a new beginning for him, a baptism of fire from which there was no turning back. He turned, and strode confidently back to his Mercedes, allowing the emergency personnel to do their jobs without his interference. As he opened the driver's side door, he glanced round once more at the ruins of the once proud citadel of his empire.

Yes, The Wraith would pay. Pay dearly.

* * * * * *

The Cobra stood smiling, confident and strong.

The Wraith began to grow weary of waiting, and all the frustration and rage that had been welling up inside him after months of fighting, searching, investigating—he lost it. The man responsible for countless deaths, unspeakable horrors and goodness knew what else, was now here, standing before him, smiling, gloating. The Wraith ran toward him, intending to break him apart. The Cobra backhanded him without taking a rearward step. The Wraith was launched backward, landing hard in the dirt a good distance from where he started.

He looked up, wiped a small trickle of blood from his bottom lip, and got to his feet, not letting the pain of that incredible blow show to his adversary. He already felt less than his best, exhausted after the incredible battles already waged, and now he faced such powerful opposition.

"Abdelkrim," The Wraith said, trying to buy himself some time. "I never thought to see you again. Not after you murdered my master and I escaped your country."

"You remember. How gratifying." The Cobra stroked his beard, his opaque eye glinting. "It is fitting you remember well the man who will grind your bones into the dust!" He pointed at him. "Kneel!"

The Wraith sensed himself falling under the Cobra's thrall. He fought valiantly but his knees began to buckle. He wavered and started to drop. He knew not to look into the

Cobra's milky eye—which resonated with a powerful, mystical energy—but couldn't help himself. The Cobra's influence was all too encompassing, especially in his weakened state.

"Unnnggghhh..." groaned the Dread Avenger as he fought with as much strength as he could muster. He had to activate the Eyes of Judgment.

"There is no use struggling. No one has ever broken my hold once I've connected. Now kneel!"

The Wraith's insides began to shake. Sweat was pouring from his brow, indeed, from every pore in his body. The Cobra had him—but he would not yield.

Strange visions inundated his mind. Images of his former life, people he knew in *both* his lives. Max, Simpson and, of course, his dear, sweet Leena. If he capitulated now, his entire life, nay lives, would have been worthless. No, he thought, he couldn't give up. He mustn't. As hard as it was, he exerted his leg muscles, and began to rise to his feet once more.

"Impossible..." the Cobra uttered.

"This city will not be taken this day," The Wraith grunted.

The Eyes of Judgment then burst to life, and their powerful energies began to counter the force from the Cobra's eye. The almost electrical battle waged for some seconds.

"I know how this ends," the Cobra said and ceased his attack. He raised his right hand, and spotlights glared on from the four corners of the pit, illuminating the construction site.

Blinding him temporarily, The Wraith suddenly heard the sound of people scrambling closer. As his vision cleared, he saw dozens of men—the Cobra's brainwashed minions, no doubt—surrounding him.

"You coward," he said. "You mean to defeat me, but you use your band of the homeless to do so. How feeble!"

Coaxing the Cobra to get angry didn't seem to work. "I will master your mind as well as your body. I want you to suffer. You have eluded me for years. Once you lie battered at my feet, perhaps then I will reveal my plans for this city—*my* city." He laughed then nodded to his men to begin their attack.

The Cobra's foot soldiers rushed forward. They were undisciplined, but they had the advantage of numbers on their side. The Wraith, fatigued from fighting all night, got to his feet. The fight was on. His fists and feet lashed out, taking down opponent after opponent. But not for long. He realized that he would soon be overcome.

No, he thought, *if I fall...* Visions of a city destroyed, of its people enslaved, his loved ones slaughtered, flooded his brain. It was Eritrea all over again. Anger welled inside him, fueled his muscles with renewed strength, gave him the power to fight back...

Willing himself to go on, The Wraith managed to beat the men back for a short time, but as he dreaded, the Cobra's army soon had him pinned down. Not yet ready to admit defeat, he nevertheless felt hollow as he remembered his thoughts of what would happen if he were to fail.

The Cobra strode toward him.

"The time has finally come, as it was fated to be." He smirked confidently. "Ready him," he ordered his men. "His will is now mine!"

The Wraith struggled as several men lifted him from the ground and stood him straight, shoving him toward their master. The Cobra's marled eye glowed once again.

"Now, Wraith, you will kneel."

The Wraith clenched his teeth, readying himself. Two cars suddenly screamed into the pit from either side, horns blaring, smashing through the barricades surrounding the building site and crashing down into the pit. Despite the substantial tumble down, both cars were still operational, and the drivers of both gunned their machines into action, horns still blaring, straight for the group congregated at the pit's center. As they neared, the intense noise forced the dozens of men to reach for their ears. The zombies scrambled, dazed and confused, as the noise began to shake the Cobra's control over them.

The Cobra turned to flee. Freed from his enemy's hold, The Wraith regained heart, and seemed to be born again with renewed strength. Both cars screeched to a halt in the dust, and Max and Leena quickly exited to help him. Now bemused by the still blaring car horns, the Cobra's men were easy targets, and the three of them fought the rabble and soon had them under strict control.

The Wraith quickly scanned the pit. The Cobra was gone.

"The Cobra, where is he?" he asked. He pushed aside Max and Leena and moved in the direction he thought the Cobra might have gone.

Max and Leena followed him.

"Thank goodness we got here in time," she said as she ran alongside him. "Max found the trail you left. I'm just so—"

The Wraith cut her off. "It's okay. For now, we have to apprehend the Cobra. He's more dangerous than ever before. We cannot fail."

The three of them climbed out of the building site and just managed to catch a glimpse of the massive frame of the Cobra turning in to a darkened alley further down the street from them. The Wraith quickened his pace.

"Hurry, we can't let him escape!" he said.

The Wraith reached the alley first, then Leena, followed by Max. It was a long alley, dark and rubbish strewn. As was common in a city as uniquely architecturally designed as

Metro City, the alley snaked and wound, branching off into smaller side alleys. Hearing the Cobra's footsteps, The Wraith knew which way to follow.

Then, rounding a final corner, the trio stopped to briefly catch their breath. There, in the distance, was the Cobra, clambering up the fire escape of a tall apartment building.

"Look!" Max shouted, pointing up to the building's roof.

There, hovering forebodingly above the building was a large airship. An elongated rope ladder dangled underneath.

The Wraith didn't dare hesitate a second longer and dashed for the fire escape. Leena moved to follow, but Max held her back.

The Wraith heard him say, "No, Leena. There's nothing we can do to help the Chief up there. He's on his own now."

The Wraith followed quickly, as he saw the Cobra disappear over the top of the building. He glanced down ever so briefly, and saw Leena and Max observing helplessly on the street below.

The Wraith was three quarters the way up the fire escape and could hear the airship beginning to move away. He pushed upward, quickening his climb as best he could. He was running on pure adrenalin, pushing his body to the limit and beyond. He reached the roof a few seconds later, just in time to see the airship floating out of reach. The rope ladder, however, was only meters from the far edge of the building. He could, he thought, just grab onto it if he made a flying leap. The distance was great, but he didn't dare think too much about it, lest the risk sway him. He sprinted for the building's edge—and jumped. Seeing he was going to fall short, he thrust his right arm out desperately, and managed to grab hold of the last rung with his fingers. Closing over the rung with fingers of steel, he gripped for sheer life, as the airship continued its flight into the night sky.

The Wraith groaned as his right shoulder strained under the pressure of stopping his fall. The Cobra had by then reached the cockpit under the immense balloon, and apparently had not yet noticed him. As the zeppelin soared, he strengthened his grip, and began to climb, his cape ballooning out around him. He didn't know how, but he knew he needed to somehow take control of the aircraft and land it safely, with its occupants his prisoners.

* * * * * *

Inside the cockpit, the Cobra stood alongside his servant, Magnus Khan, and Natalie Black, the pretty receptionist from the City Morgue, who piloted the aircraft.

"Well done, Natalya, our escape has been perfectly planned," the Cobra said.

"Master, we have failed," Khan said.

The Cobra backhanded him, sending the hapless underling to the floor by Black's side. "I do not fail—ever! We are simply falling back and will again strike forward terribly when the time is right. True, The Wraith somehow managed to ascertain a way to break my sway over those cretins sooner than I had anticipated, but that changes nothing. It only delays the inevitable." Khan, chagrined, stood silently. "We will now head for our valley stronghold, where nothing and no one will stop me from taking what is mine. It is my destiny to conquer, and I will fulfill that promise."

Ignoring Khan and Black, the Cobra moved over to the side window, and stood silently with his back to them. Black, real name Natalya Blackova, former Soviet operative, before falling willingly under his influence, piloted the airship skillfully up over the enormous expanse that was Metro City.

In minutes, they would be sailing over the outer suburbs of the city, and on toward the nearby escarpment, to a place unknown to anyone but themselves.

No one would find them.

~ Chapter 28 ~

The airship sped onward, up through the clouds, causing Blackova to rely on her instruments to navigate the craft. It was a cloudy night, with storms forecast to barrel down upon the city on the morrow. Khan sat in the chair beside Blackova, while the Cobra continued staring out the window.

Just then, The Wraith burst into the cockpit. Khan was the first to meet him.

"Time for round two," The Wraith said.

Khan growled as he began the battle, and while The Wraith's strength had been diluted, his anger, his determination, obeyed his commands more than ever before. Where Khan had been close to his physical equal in their previous encounter, his anger now knew no bounds. Evading each of Khan's blows, The Wraith lashed out, ending the battle with one powerful strike.

Blackova dared not react, for the craft just experienced some slight turbulence, and she needed her full attention directed to piloting it. Her master was on his own.

"Abdelkrim!" The Wraith boomed. "You will not escape me again. I have not forgotten your atrocities in Africa."

The Cobra growled with fury, and they battled there, in the cramped zeppelin cockpit, not only for their lives, but the lives of everyone in Metro City! The struggle was fierce, with neither quarry gaining any advantage. Blows of inconceivable force were blocked and traded. There wasn't much room to evade between men of such size, and both combatants were soon showing the evidence of their battle. The Cobra finally lashed out with a strong uppercut, which slammed The Wraith into the wall opposite. Blood was splattered on the faces of both warriors, as they paused briefly, eyeing each other off.

"It is fitting to finish this here, above your beloved city," the Cobra said slowly. "We are the only two worthy to hold her in his hands." Then, as if in afterthought, he added, "After our previous encounters; after what you did to me, it is indeed fitting to fight for her here in the stratosphere."

The Wraith wiped the blood from under his nose, stepped forward. "You let others fight your battles; you flee like the coward you are. I did nothing to you. You *are* nothing! Metro City will never be yours."

"Then let us finish this now."

He launched himself at The Wraith, whose speed now failed him, and slammed into him, sending them both careening into the far wall. The Wraith grunted in pain as the Cobra reached for his throat, attempting to squeeze the life from him.

"You gave me this power I have," the Cobra snarled. "It was my destiny to receive everything from the old man."

The Wraith reached up, trying to break free from the villain's iron grip. "You were not worthy then...you are still not worthy."

The Cobra, furious, pulled him forward, never lessening his grip on his throat. The Cobra slammed him back into the wall. He did this two more times, with The Wraith getting closer to unconsciousness with each blow. The Cobra did so for a fourth time, but this time the wall failed to hold under the incredible force smashing into it.

The Wraith and the Cobra plummeted out into the cold night, falling to their doom.

* * * * * *

Max and Leena raced through the city traffic in their car, but it was hopeless. Leena had insisted they follow the path of the airship, with Max craning his head out the window, trying to keep it in view, but once the craft had vanished up through the clouds, it was impossible to see where the ship was or where it was heading.

"I'm sorry, Leena, but we didn't get enough of a view to see where she was going," Max said, looking downcast. "They could have been heading for the mountains but could easily have been headed elsewhere."

Leena parked the car abruptly at the nearest free spot and stared at him.

"Then..." she started, but remembered Paul's training, remembered to control herself in situations of dire importance. No matter how bad things looked, she needed to keep control. Paul would have wanted it that way. "We head home," she said, "and we monitor things from the Lair. At least from there we may be able to ascertain the airship's direction."

Max smiled.

Leena turned in to the traffic and steered in the direction of home.

* * * * * *

The Wraith and the Cobra plunged through the icy air. The Wraith knew there was no hope of using his cloak to float to safety, not at this velocity. The only hope of survival was if he reached out for the ladder before it was too late. He had to move—*now*! Using his left arm—the stronger of the two since injuring his right in the leap for the rope ladder earlier—he grabbed the last rung and screamed in pain as his shoulder dislocated from its socket. Somehow his fingers held tight, and in agony, held firm. Seconds later, the Cobra whizzed down past him and in one last desperate grab for survival, latched on to The Wraith's ankle. The Wraith screamed. He couldn't hang on with the added burden of someone the size and weight of the Cobra. Before his hand gave way, he thrust his right hand up and gripped the rung. His left arm dangled lifelessly by his side. He knew he couldn't hold for long under the load of two large, heavily muscled men.

The Wraith looked down and managed to catch a glimpse of his adversary staring up at him. The Cobra peered up with mocking eyes, struggling to maintain his grip on his enemy's ankle. The Cobra then grinned, as if he knew fate had somehow dealt him a different hand.

"Did I not say it was fitting," the Cobra shouted above the noise of the wind and the airship's engine, "to end this here? Indeed, though it is not the end I anticipated."

As his words were drowned out by the stark winds, his grip on The Wraith's ankle faltered...

...and he fell.

He never screamed on the way down.

The Wraith, his body battered and bruised, pulled himself up and gripped the ladder rung under his right elbow. At least he was safe...for the time being.

Suddenly, the airship began to swerve, as if trying to shake him off. The Wraith realized that either one or both of the two above in the cockpit knew the Cobra was lost and was trying to gain retribution by shaking him off. He held tight with his remaining strength, but it was tough with the swaying of the aircraft and the now high wind threatening to loosen him from his perch. As impossible as the situation seemed with his injuries, he had to make his way back up to the cockpit. Slowly but surely, as the airship buffeted in the storm, The Wraith struggled to the top. Finally, he staggered inside the cockpit, and saw Khan still prone on the floor.

Natalya Blackova remained at the helm of the airship, now rocking wildly, due both to the impact of the storm and to her mad attempts at revenge against The Wraith. The Wraith's mind reeled—what was he to do? Take control of the ship, of course, but he knew it wouldn't be an easy task, and he barely had the strength to stand, let alone potentially engage in another battle. Did she even know he had returned to the cockpit? Perhaps he could surprise her and end this with little effort.

Before he had a chance to conceive a plan of action, let alone to act, Blackova whirled and fired a high-powered pistol at him. "Die!"

The Wraith scarcely managed to evade the initial barrage, but the bullets kept coming, and one found its mark in his upper right thigh, shattering his femur. The Wraith shouted in anguish, retreated, slipping back through the large opening caused by his previous battle with the Cobra. He gained a firm hold at the top of the ladder. Gaining control of the ship, landing it safely, was no longer an option, not in his physical condition, and staying aboard the cockpit was now clearly impossible. As it was, he could hardly consider what course of action to take next; his pain was indescribable.

No sooner had he lamented the current situation, the zeppelin banked downward sharply. He could barely hang on. The airship careened down through the clouds and the Gladstone skyline quickly became visible.

The Wraith was helpless as Blackova madly banked the ship down, aiming for the tallest building in their vicinity. *Is she so mad as to sacrifice her own life just to gain revenge upon me?* The Wraith's mind raced.

The Wraith dangled there, his left shoulder badly torn from its socket, his right shoulder strained to the limit, blood flowing from wounds to the face and thigh. He tried to gather his thoughts. It couldn't end this way. To have defeated the greatest evil he had ever known, only for his own end to come so soon after victory—no, not now.

With the ship dangerously close to the building, it banked upward sharply, sending the rope ladder toward the building at great speed. The Wraith swiftly knew there was only one hope. A slim one perhaps, but...sliding down the ladder as far he could, he prepared himself. Seeing a window close by, he let go of the ladder and crashed through it and a desk behind it, before smashing into the wall at the far end of the empty office.

He lay there, finally able to rest. He survived. He wasn't sure how, but he was alive. Unconsciousness beckoned, and in the seconds he had remaining, he thought to himself—*knew*—that despite what he'd been through, it had been worth it. The Cobra had been defeated; a great pall had been lifted from the city. To save his city, to rescue innocents, he would sacrifice all, even his own life, in his endless war against evil. This day, he had survived, though barely, and while some had escaped, the Cobra himself had perished in battle.

As these thoughts drifted through his mind, blackness began to envelope him.

~ Epilogue Part 2 ~

Paul woke suddenly and winced in pain as he tried to sit. His left arm was in a sling and heavily bandaged. His hands were also bandaged and his right leg was covered in a tight plaster cast. He felt weak and while he could tell he was under the influence of painkillers, the pain was still evident.

Leena appeared with a breakfast tray.

"Oh, you're awake," she said with surprise. "Dr. Needham and I hoped you might be ready for some solids today, so I brought you up some broth to start with."

Paul smiled at her. As always, she looked so beautiful and her presence seemed to lessen the pain a little. He tried to motion to her with his right arm, but noticed it was restricted by the attachment of a drip.

"How...how bad is it?" he managed to ask, his voice a weak rasp.

Leena lay down the tray on the bedside table and sat beside him. "Your left shoulder was badly mangled; we didn't think it would ever heal, initially. But Dr. Needham seems to think there's hope, with intensive physiotherapy, that you'll regain most, if not all, your strength back in time. Your thigh will heal. Your other injuries are minimal under the circumstances."

Leena gazed at him lovingly, though with a worried edge to her expression.

Don't worry, Paul thought. He knew the risks he undertook in the life he had chosen, knew it was all or nothing, but he had supreme confidence, not only in Dr. Needham's surgical abilities, but those of his own amazing recuperative powers.

He smiled at her. "How long have I been out?"

"A week has passed since your battle with the Cobra, since Max and I hauled you out of that office. We'd lost you once that airship moved above the clouds but we were able to track your progress from the Lair. We're just lucky you weren't too far from home and we were able to get to the building you wound up in before anyone else could find you." She took a deep breath before continuing. "You've drifted in and out of consciousness since then though I'm not surprised you don't remember much with those painkillers Dr. Needham has you on."

"And the airship?"

"We're not sure. I thought they were heading for the escarpment, but as Max said, they really could have gone anywhere. We lost sight of them once we tracked you down." Leena paused briefly. "I'm sorry, Paul."

Paul wanted so badly to take her in his arms, to tell her how much he loved her, to tell her everything was okay, but he was too dizzy from sitting up, so leaned back against the headboard. Leena propped a couple of pillows behind him, making him more comfortable, and returned his smile.

"Do you feel up for some of my broth?"

Paul gazed into her beautiful blue eyes. "I'm starving."

Leena began spooning the broth carefully into his mouth. Though nourished via the drip, it wasn't the same as proper food and his stomach was aching from the lack of it.

After the last spoonful, Paul again gazed into her eyes. "I love you, Leena."

She bent over to kiss Paul. He was satisfied. Despite his great personal cost receiving horrendous, almost crippling injuries, it was worth it. The city was safe. He would heal now. But he knew evil would not rest. When it showed itself again, as it no doubt would too soon, woe be to anyone who would dare face The Wraith.

VALLEY OF EVIL

~ Sneak peek ~

Turn the page for a preview of the next novel in the series,
Valley of Evil, by Frank Dirscherl.

AVAILABLE NOW from Trinity Comics

~ Chapter 1 ~

The expansive grounds of the estate of Metro City's latest player in crime, Ma Tzi, were patrolled by several burly, armed guards. All appeared well equipped and to be the kind to shoot first and ask questions later. As they patrolled, they gripped their weapons tightly, straining to see in the darkness of the warm, late spring night.

Crouched in a nearby grove of shrubbery, The Wraith and his assistant, Max Horton, watched on intently, waiting for their opportunity to move. Max glanced over to The Wraith for any sign, but there was none. The Wraith remained crouched, his eyes squinting with concentration through narrow slits, his muscles flexed and ready for action—a jungle predator stalking its prey.

As the patrols moved away from their vantage point, a thin, tight smile appeared on The Wraith's lips. He motioned to Max, and they made their move, leaving the safety of their darkened hideaway. The two sped forth, sprinting effortlessly for a medium-sized bungalow alongside the estate's Olympic-sized swimming pool. Ma Tzi, the self-proclaimed Dragon of his empire—a drug lord—had made Metro City his home in the months since the city's partial destruction at the hands of the Cobra. Resident crime lord Robert Latham's empire had taken a strong hit then, and Tzi, the Hong Kong expatriate who already had control of the drug trade of several cities on the West Coast of the US, had seen his opportunity to take control from a rival he no doubt perceived to be weak and vulnerable.

What he found, however, was far from that. True, Latham's empire had suffered somewhat during the Cobra's offensive against the city, but Latham could hardly be described as weak. Metro City had been wracked with an intense urban war between the two crime factions. For months, attacks both subtle and overt had been made by both sides, with neither gaining any real advantage. The Wraith had watched on, unable to intervene due to the serious injuries he sustained in defeating the Cobra and his army of the homeless, but now that he had healed, he had to take action, lest his city fall waste to the war now being waged.

The Wraith and Max reached the front of the bungalow quickly and hunched down tight against the front wall. Their actions remained undetected, and they were alone in the black shadows of the night. Max removed from his back a small backpack and pulled from it night-vision goggles and a small lock-pick.

"With the alarm already disabled," Max whispered, "this'll be a cinch. In-and-out." He put on the goggles.

"Open the door, quickly," The Wraith whispered tersely.

Max had the door open in an instant, and the duo crept inside the darkened abode. The Wraith pressed against his cowl at his right temple and special night-vision lenses dropped into place over his eyes. Max was The Wraith's chief assistant in his war on crime, and also his mechanic, chauffeur and inventor of all the gadgets he used in his struggle against evil. These special lenses were but a small fraction of the equipment at The Wraith's disposal.

The interior of the bungalow appeared as expected. It was one large open-plan room filled with pool and garden equipment. Max shuffled forward through the room then turned to face The Wraith.

"Chief, you sure your intel was on the money?" Max asked softly.

The Wraith silently walked past him and moved along a side window. Ignoring Max, he ran his fingers under the window ledge until he reached a spot at the bottom left-hand corner. A section of the floor adjacent to the window slid open, revealing a narrow staircase burrowing down into a black abyss.

"I'm sure," The Wraith said.

Max joined The Wraith in standing before the staircase. With their night-vision lenses in place, they could see the stairs journey down into the unknown, though in this case, they knew exactly where it led.

"You sure you don't want me down there with you?" Max asked.

"I need you to stay here and stand point. Tzi's men could come along this way at any moment, and I need you here to distract them long enough for me to get the job done and for us to escape."

Max looked at The Wraith with concerned eyes, but said nothing. The Wraith knew Max well enough to know that despite his assistant's concerns, Max would follow him at his word, every time.

The Wraith dropped into the darkness, leaving Max to stand guard. The Wraith had received a tip-off from his contact within Tzi's camp that, unlike most crime lords, Tzi kept most of his operations close to home. In this case, his major drug distillation plant was located right under his own estate, in a secret and well-secured underground den. The audacity of the drug lord didn't fail to gall the Dread Avenger of the Underworld.

A few seconds passed before The Wraith reached the bottom of the stairs, where he was met by a large, and obviously sturdy, door. To the left of the door about chest high was an intricate security keypad. The Wraith's contact had given him the access code. He keyed it in. Success.

The door slid open with a whoosh of gears as the lights strobed on automatically. The Wraith quickly retracted his night-vision lenses and took in the incredible sight before him. It was as though he were standing on the floor of an enormous warehouse. Canisters were carefully stacked four-high in innumerable rows on either side, stretching all the way to the far wall. In the center was Tzi's laboratory equipment, no doubt for discovering new, more addictive drugs to flood the city—indeed the country—with. The Wraith clenched his jaw. Tzi hadn't wasted any time in the months since he invaded Metro City; The Wraith partially blamed himself for the apparent ease at which Tzi had made the city his home. He had been badly wounded in his battle with the Cobra, and had required months of recuperation and rehabilitation. Even now, though stronger and well-healed, he still felt twinges of pain every now and then, and he damned the fates that had brought this new evil to his city.

He focused on the task at hand. From his belt he removed several small explosive nodes and scanned the warehouse for strategic points to plant them. Moving deftly amongst the evidence of Tzi's evil, The Wraith hastily secured the nodules in various places throughout the entirety of the warehouse.

The Wraith retreated swiftly, and made sure to close the warehouse door behind him, securing it in place. He leaped up the stairs three at a time, and soon returned to Max, still stationed as he was by the door of the bungalow.

"Everything's in place. The explosives are set on a ten-minute fuse. Get ready to get out of here," The Wraith whispered.

As they began to open the door, a multitude of small arms fire reverberated across the grounds of the estate. Max shut the door tight and looked at him. He motioned Max to remain quiet and took his place by the door. He opened the door ever so slightly, just enough to peek out into the night. What he saw was nothing short of full-blown warfare—Tzi's men raced around in panic, firing wildly in all directions. Something or someone had caused them to react like this and The Wraith knew it could only be Robert Latham, launching yet another offensive against his arch rival. His mind buzzed with a strategy to not only escape their current position—for it was potentially about to disintegrate in an explosion of intense fury—but to take advantage of the disarray caused by Latham's attack.

The Wraith smiled.

"You've got something planned, I can see it," Max said as the sounds of battle raged ever stronger.

"This is going to be a night both Latham and Tzi will never forget."

They waited for their chance, then, when the raging battle outside seemed to have moved away from them, they quickly slipped out into the night.

* * * * * *

Inside his massive mansion stronghold, Ma Tzi was anxious. He was the average height of a Chinese male, with very short black hair, and such smooth skin as to almost defy his middle age. Tzi sat in a large room filled with monitors where he ordinarily saw almost every corner of his estate. Several, however, were blacked out. Tzi remained seated while his men worked frantically, trying to re-establish the connections.

"Hurry!" the crime lord yelled, his English carrying only a hint of a Chinese accent. "I must know what is happening. I must be able to co-ordinate my defenses."

"Power to sections seven and eight have been cut. We haven't been able to restore them yet," replied one eager young employee.

Tzi stood. He felt the veins in his temples throbbing with fury. "Damn you, Mr. Latham! Why won't you sit down and accept the inevitable?" he asked, more of himself than to his staff. "Why won't you accept my gracious offer and join me? Surely you must realize this action is fruitless? Surely you must realize the only way you can survive in this city is to work for me!"

Tzi walked over to the communications hub of his surveillance center and barked orders to his men outside, who battled to stave off the invasion by Latham's forces.

"Push them back, my warriors," Tzi commanded in his smooth, cultured yet deep voice. "This is but another of Mr.

Latham's 'exploratory actions.' Deal with them as you have in the past!"

Tzi turned and faced his surveillance crew. He smiled and returned to his seat.

"Now, please restore the power to sections seven and eight as quickly as possible. I do not wish to be caught off guard again."

* * * * * *

The Wraith had ordered Max to safety, then continued through the Tzi estate. Now with this conflagration having started, The Wraith thought one man could squeeze through the intense defenses where two could not, and above all, he had a much more important job for Max to accomplish, one which only Max and Leena could do while he remained here in this stronghold of evil. He listened, and knew the site of the battle had shifted to the northern-most extent of Tzi's estate. Latham's forces were being pushed back, as they had been in their previous attempts. Still, The Wraith thought, this kind of work was better done alone. He crept toward the main mansion. Flattening himself against the wall of the superb Mandarin-designed structure, he inched toward the corner, and carefully peered around. Spying the front door, he saw it well-guarded by at least four armed men. The Wraith pulled back and thought for a moment. Entering the house, even one as well protected as this one, was relatively easy for him, but sneaking inside undetected was, this time, not his intended purpose. He wanted in, and to make an impact in doing so. So, that left the front entrance which, despite the danger, suited him perfectly.

The four guards watched and waited for any signs of movement. They were prepared, it seemed, for any eventuality, and would rebuke any invasion with brute force. *But they're not prepared for me,* The Wraith thought. They remained still, appearing to be following the sounds of gunfire moving away. One turned to face the other and in doing so saw what the others did not.

The Wraith dropped behind them, raising his cloak.

"Holy!" the guard cried out, raising his weapon, ready to fire at the Dread Avenger.

The Wraith grabbed the smallest of the four hapless guards from behind and tossed him at the guard who was about to shoot. With both of them temporarily out of action, The Wraith settled his attention toward the other two.

One of the remaining guards was able to raise his weapon toward him, but The Wraith caught the gun and pushed it skyward. The gun went off. The Wraith delivered a powerful blow to the guard's stomach, sending him to his knees. The other guard swung at him with his weapon, but The Wraith rolled swiftly to one side, only catching a glimpse as the swinging weapon smacked into the other guard—who was on his knees—knocking him out. On his feet in an instant, The Wraith executed a leg-sweep, sending the standing guard to the ground hard. A karate chop ended the battle. The Wraith turned and glared at the first two guards lying close to him. They were awake and had watched the fight with fear in their eyes. Their weapons were lost.

"Leave—NOW!" The Wraith ordered as the Eyes of Judgment on his chest began to crackle with energy, gleaming a sickening yellow. Fearful for their lives, the two guards stood—and ran!

The Wraith spun on his heels and made his way to the front door. He had a message for Tzi this night, and nothing would prevent him from delivering it. As he reached the porch, two more guards streamed forth from the house. The

Wraith dealt each of them powerful blows to the face without breaking stride, rendering them unconscious. He entered the Tzi mansion and saw the ornate Chinese décor throughout. Knowing the floor plan of the house to perfection—*Know thy enemy*, thought The Wraith—he marched through the maze of rooms, encountering more guards along the way. He made quick work of all of them.

*   *   *   *   *   *

Inside his surveillance center, the Dragon looked on with concern. He had been happy as he watched Latham's men fall back, happy as his warriors—as he so described them—had once again repelled the horde of his enemy. Now, however, he had heard the shots from close by and knew that something was amiss. The cameras had failed to pick anything up except shadows...and that worried him. Normally a cool and calm man, with an almost kindly disposition, Tzi nevertheless realized the potential damage Latham, or others, could do while he was not in total control of his surroundings, which he always had been when seated here. His men milled about, continuing to frantically work to bring the power back up to various parts of the estate, but it was slow going. Latham's forces had done a stellar job, and only so much could be done in this central control base before other repair work had to be done elsewhere. Tzi sat motionless, his mind reeling, thinking of a way to make Latham pay dearly for this transgression.

In an instant, the relative calm of the room was shattered by an explosion which blew the room's double-door completely off, careening it forward. It slammed into some of the intricate computer equipment. A pall of smoke erupted from the shattered doorway. The room's occupants had been thrown back against the far wall behind Tzi, who remained in his seat. For interminable seconds, silence reigned. Then, emerging from the smoke, appearing briefly as though some creature from hell appeared two shimmering, eerie lights instantly preceding the imposing form of The Wraith.

"Men of the Dragon, hear me now!" The Wraith boomed. "Your days in my city are numbered. Know that I am watching you, watching every move you make, and I will not allow you to turn her into your own personal battlefield."

Tzi's bottom lip quivered and contorted with anger as he listened to every word.

"Your time is coming, Tzi," The Wraith said. "Today marks the beginning of your downfall, and I promise you, neither you nor Robert Latham will come out of this unscathed!"

At this Tzi stood sharply, as though about to reply with a threat of his own, but he stopped himself as The Wraith seemed to almost float backward, unearthly, back into the still-billowing smoke. And in moments, he was gone.

"Find him! No one threatens the Dragon and lives!" Tzi snarled.

Before anyone could move to respond, the room shook to the ferocity of a massive explosion. The lights and monitors flickered briefly before cutting out completely, plunging the room into darkness. The shaking stopped, but panic filled the surveillance room.

"Be calm, be calm," Tzi commanded, but even the Dragon could not control his men's fear. "Find out where that explosion came from."

The men rushed for the door, seemingly ignoring his command, fleeing as fast as they could. Tzi was forced to follow, and he loped through the maze of rooms of his self-styled Chinese paradise toward the house's front door.

Out in the night, what he saw shocked even his jaded eyes. Despite the explosion having taken place a mere two minutes ago, a massive ball of flame was still shooting skyward from where the pool-side bungalow once stood, and through the intense inferno, he could see the gigantic hole through which the flames spewed. Tzi knew at once that his drug lab would never be operational again and he was filled with an anger he had only ever felt once before, back in Hong Kong when his parents had been murdered by English officials when he was just a child. He knew this was the work of The Wraith. He looked up to the barely visible stars and swore vengeance.

* * * * * *

Robert Latham sat at the desk of his eccentrically furnished study, surrounded by the busts of the dictators he so admired—Caesar, Mussolini, Napoleon, George W. Bush, Donald Trump and others—as he received news of his forces now retreating from battle.

No matter, he thought, sniffing indignantly, as he listened on the phone. Once finished, he lay the phone back into its cradle. Every incursion he ordered was merely to ascertain weak points in Tzi's armor. Latham knew there were such weak spots, knew they must exist, and was determined to find them no matter the cost or sacrifice. He wasn't about to let some outsider step into his city, meddle with his personal property, and do as he pleased. No, this would not be allowed, and whatever the cost, he would prevail over his newest enemy. If need be, he would fight his war on two fronts—against Tzi and against The Wraith...and he would win.

He turned in his chair and gazed out his large bay window, out onto his lawn, watching the lights of the city glittering in the background. *The city...my city.* He had done much to repair what the Cobra had wrought. In some small way, he felt it his job to make amends to the city which he had helped bring to partial destruction by calling in the Cobra in the first place. In doing so, he not only contributed to the deaths of countless thousands, but that of his own daughter as well. Despite these horrors, strangely, he felt no great sense of remorse, as he deemed them all casualties of war. A war he must win.

He breathed heavily and spun back around to face his desk. Getting back to his paperwork, he began signing several important documents when he heard a tap at his window. He looked up with surprise, and turned to face The Wraith, staring at him through the bay window. Though shocked, Latham didn't budge. The Wraith raised his hand to the window, his fingers pressing against it. With a loud crash, shattered glass showered over Latham and throughout the study. Latham shielded his eyes from the shards.

A thick haze wafted into the study, courtesy of a gas pellet lobbed into the room. Latham coughed and hacked as he brushed the bits of glass from his suit. Blinded by the smoke, he froze, waiting for what he thought would be an inevitable attack. It didn't come. Instead, the familiar booming tone of The Wraith's voice beckoned.

"Latham, your sins against humanity have continued tonight. They will cease, or I will wreck unmitigated harm upon you. You surely realize I speak the truth and are aware of the consequences!"

Latham sputtered as the smoke finally began to dissipate. There was no one to reply to. The Wraith had gone...and Latham was alone.

~ Sneak peek ~

Turn the page for a preview of the next novel in the series,
Vendetta, by Frank Dirscherl.

COMING SOON from Trinity Comics

~ Chapter 1 ~

Robert Latham strode into the ornately designed and furnished study in his Metro City home and moved over to the deep mahogany sideboard and poured himself a Cognac from the crystal decanter there. He sniffed, drank, and gazed at his surrounds. Decorated in much the same fashion as his city office, there were busts of the world leaders throughout history that he so admired. For their strength, their cunning. Their ruthlessness. Caesar, Genghis Khan, Stalin, Mao Ze Dong, George W. Bush and Donald Trump were but some of the specimens there. He took another drink, the delicious Remy Martin clarifying his thoughts, and headed to his desk.

Taking a seat in the plush buttoned leather chair, he hadn't a moment to relax before the phone rang.

"Yes?" he said, indignantly. "Oh, Patrich. Good of you to call. What news?"

He took another sip from his drink, savoring the taste while listening.

"You've dealt with Jones, then? Excellent. Oh dear...another deputy with delusions of grandeur. At least Charlie had some sense of patience, and bided his time before trying anything. I spared Charlie for that reason. He may not have been loyal but at least he was halfway competent. But Jones...he never had a chance." Latham leaned back in his chair and smiled. "You're not going to get any similar ideas now are you, Patrich? I wouldn't be very pleased to have to do away with three deputies in a row. My reputation would take a battering." He paused. "Good, smart boy. Good work tonight, also. Efficient and deadly. Traits I admire. You can go home now. We have a busy day tomorrow."

He hung up before any response could be received.

Leaning forward, he chuckled briefly while reaching for the alabaster cigar case on his desk. As he opened the lid and reached inside, the light instantly dimmed to almost nothing, and a screen dropped down from the ceiling at the far end of the room.

"What the...?!"

"Now, now," a familiar voice emanated seemingly from nowhere and everywhere all at once.

"Charlie?" Latham said, with a mixture of bemusement and anger. "How the he—?"

"Temper, temper," Charlie Grieco said, as his face flashed upon the large screen. Latham's former deputy appeared as always; slickly dressed with a smarmy, arrogant air about him. "Is that any way to greet your old comrade?" He laughed while talking.

"What's going on here, Charlie? How did you get this stuff in here?"

Grieco grinned. "Can the great Robert Latham have forgotten that I was his right-hand man for nearly ten years? That I know all his secrets, inside and out?"

"I changed every passcode, altered all my security procedures as I always do after every..." Latham wheezed.

"Purge?" Grieco chimed in. "Is that how you were about to explain your betrayal of me?"

Latham fumed. "Betrayal of you?! You little worm! You tried to usurp control of my organization for yourself. Thought yourself the new big man of Metro City."

"Because you wouldn't let go!" Grieco screamed. "You didn't know when to step aside and let some fresh blood taste their fair share of power. You delayed me from my destiny. And now it's going to cost you."

Latham recovered his composure, leaned back and lit his cigar, blowing smoke before continuing. "Cost me? You must be insane. I don't know where you are or how you managed to pull this off, but you're a dead man, you hear me. A dead man!"

"Funny," Grieco replied, his smile never leaving him, "I was thinking the same thing about you. You asked before how I managed to achieve my little show for you in your study there. Well, I can't take all the credit, you know. I had a little bit of help. I bumped into an old friend of ours, you see. With my knowledge of your practices, and his...well, his skills, we were able to..."

"Get to the point, Charlie," Latham snapped.

"Hmm...well, why don't I let him tell you about it then."

Grieco stepped out of camera range and was quickly replaced by another man, one Latham knew all too well. Crossfire!

He's alive, Latham thought, genuinely frightened for the first time in his life. *How is this possible?*

His tall, muscular frame filled the screen with an imposing menace. His long blond hair was in a ponytail as it was the last time they had met, and there was that annoying little cross-hairs tattoo on the left side of his neck, but he appeared different as well, outfitted in a formfitting black bodysuit, with bullet pouches crisscrossing both shoulders. Emblazoned at the top of his chest was a small duplicate image of the tattoo, in white, with a smeared, blood-red center dot. As the villain leaned in close to the camera, his heavily tanned and lined face became clearer.

"Latham...by your expression I see you remember me."

Latham found it difficult to breathe. Charlie Grieco and Crossfire, teaming up, somehow able to penetrate the security of his home.

"You're no doubt wondering how I come to be alive, how and why I've teamed up with our mutual friend here," he said, gesturing off camera. "The why I'm sure you can work out for yourself. As to the first question...you're going to take that one unanswered to your grave."

Latham gulped, sweat pouring down his brow. He tried to move but was paralyzed with fear, a feeling completely alien to him. "But, but...my family, don't..."

Grieco re-appeared on the screen to stand alongside the much larger Crossfire, the latter of which produced a small apparatus from his belt.

"Goodbye," Crossfire breathed, while Grieco cackled, pressing a button on the apparatus.

A burst of fiery light shot forth, and then...

Darkness.

* * * * * *

The Latham mansion exploded in an inferno that was almost akin to a nuclear detonation. In seconds, the massive house was reduced to mere rubble, and flames spewed skyward as though the Devil's domain was attempting an invasion of Heaven itself. In minutes, with the sirens of the emergency crews sounding in the distance, the conflagration grew, spreading throughout the grounds of the estate. There was no stopping it.

Crossfire's vengeance had been complete. And satisfied.

* * * * * *

Grieco couldn't contain his joy. He shrieked and danced about like a nerd prancing at the prom with the head cheerleader.

"I did it," he shouted. "He's gone. The old man is finally history, and I'm free to take over the organization. Finally to lead."

He turned to face his new found ally. Crossfire stared back at him with a stern expression belying any joy he might have felt at their success.

"Why so glum?" Grieco said, oblivious to anything other than his own ecstasy. "Your enemy is dead. Your mission is complete. Now you can go home to Cobar, or wherever it was you said you came from. Unless, of course, you want a job in *my* organization. I could use a man with your...skills."

Crossfire remained motionless, merely staring at Grieco for some further seconds before finally speaking. "You think my mission is over? That killing Latham is all that I desire?"

"Well, I...I don't know, I..." Grieco stammered, finally starting to think that the situation may not be quite as he imagined. He took a few steps back.

"Latham was just the beginning," Crossfire barked. "And you were simply a means to an end. And now it is your end."

Grieco gulped. Crossfire lifted a gauntletted arm, smirked, and fired.

* * * * * *

Lead coughed from the miniature automatic weapon secreted within the fabric of the arm of his suit. A powerful uzi-style weapon, it connected with the bullets strapped around his bulky frame, meaning it unlikely he would ever run out of bullets in the short term.

The barrage of bullets tore Grieco's body to shreds. When Crossfire finally relented, bloody pieces of flesh were strewn at his feet. He didn't care. As he had said—a means to an end. All his enemies would suffer the same fate. However, Grieco's remains, and Latham's demise, would send a message to the one enemy he was *really* after. The one who deserved every torture, every cruelty, and then finally, death, more than any other.

The Wraith.

~ Interview with Frank Dirscherl ~

Q: What was the first story you ever wrote?

A: Way back in primary school, fourth grade, I think, it was a short writing project I did based on a *Daredevil* comic I had recently read. I was immensely proud of it at the time, though I can't imagine it was any good. My first story for publication was the script for *The Wraith #1* comic book and my first prose work was the novel *The Wraith*.

Q: Where do you get your ideas from?

A: From life. From my wife Jennifer, from work, from friends, from what I read, from what I see. As others far more famous and eloquent than I have long said...if you wish to write about life, you need to experience it. Travel, read everything you can get your hands on. Enlighten yourselves on subjects beyond your limited interests. Open your eyes to the world, not just what's happening in your own backyard.

Q: What style of book or comic book do you prefer?

A: Oh, I like bits and pieces of everything, there isn't one set style or type of written work that I like best. I love well written novels. I'm a *huge* Sherlock Holmes fan, so I suppose my favorite books are Holmes books (and movies, TV shows etc.), be they the official canon by Sir Arthur Conan Doyle or some of the better written pastiches (eg. those by Barrie Roberts, Donald Thomas, Val Andrews and John Hall, for example). I'm also a very big fan of Agatha Christie's Poirot series of books (and movies, TV shows etc.). I like adventure books, fantasy books, science fiction books, pulp novels (such as the Spider, the Shadow etc.), comic books, even children's books (the Hardy Boys, Three Investigators, Harry Potter etc.). I also like a large variety of non-fiction work (books about Jack the Ripper, Arthur Conan Doyle, Winston Churchill, Frederick Barbarossa and many, many more). I also enjoy reading film screenplays (particularly superhero films), magazines, newspapers and more. My favorite comic book? Again, I have many favorites, but I guess my favorite style is the comic book from the 70s - early 80s, with the work of the 50s and 60s just a slight rung below. What all these eras have in common is the vast amount of fun, of pure entertainment, comics supplied during those times, and which seems mostly lost from the industry today.

Q: Who are your favorite authors?

A: Well, some are listed in my previous answer, but some more of my favorites are as follows (not in order): Sir Arthur Conan Doyle, Barrie Roberts, Donald Thomas, David Stuart Davies, Agatha Christie, Ron Fortier, Bobby Nash, Norvell Page, Raymond Chandler and some others.

Q: Where did you get the idea for The Wraith?

A: The Wraith is my way of combining the worlds of the pulp novel with that of the kinds of comic book that I grew up reading in the 70s and 80s—for example, the superb comic books written by the likes of Dennis O'Neil, Steve Englehart, Len Wein, Gerry Conway and Marv Wolfman. Being a huge fan of both forms of literature, I thought it might be a cool thing to try and combine the two, and that's how The Wraith was born in 1998. As the years went on, and I became more and more disillusioned with the current comic book storytelling from the major publishers (DC & Marvel), I was able to fully flesh out the character and decided to make a go of it in the comic book and prose novel arena. Since then I've done several comic books, novels, non-fiction works and a live-action movie. The sky's the limit for this character!

Q: How long will *The Wraith Adventures* series of books continue?

A: Indefinitely. As long as I have ideas for books, the series will continue. As the character is my creation, I feel I have the best handle on him and his world. And my head is bursting with ideas. I already have several books ahead plotted, so off we go.

Q: What are your regular habits as a writer?

A: I don't have any. Pure and simple. As writing is not a profession for me (I have a job as a librarian, which I've had for more than twenty five years!), I only write when I feel the passion for it. Writing is a true passion project for me. Which is why I can go months, sometimes years, without writing one word. If I don't feel the urge to write, I don't. Simple as that. I don't force myself to write. That's typical writer BS that I just don't—can't—follow. If I don't feel it, I don't fake it.

Oh, I guess there is one thing I sometimes do. I occasionally keep notes, but not a whole lot. Sometimes I outline, if you want to call it that, in point form, and sometimes I write a novel (or portions of it, at least) in long form, just because I sometimes want to get away from sitting at a computer (those things bug me at times), and I find writing by hand relaxes me.

About the Type

Garamond is a group of many old-style serif typefaces, originally those designed by Parisian craftsman Claude Garamond and other 16th century French engravers, and now many modern revivals. Though his name was written as 'Garamont' in his lifetime, the typefaces are generally spelled 'Garamond'. **Garamond Normal**, used in this book, is one of those modern revivals.

The Wraith in his original print costume. Art by John Jett

The Wraith letting the Cobra have it. Art by Jim Taylor
and Jeff Austin

The Wraith character sheet. Art by Jeff Austin

Cobra design sketches. Art by Roland Bird

Cobra Rough Sketches.

Cobra design sketches. Art by Roland Bird

LEENA

John 11/02

Leena Patterson design sketch. Art by John Jett

Natalya Blackova design sketches. Art by Roland Bird

The director/co-writer, Stephen J. Semones, posing in front of
a green-screen with the film's star, David Cooper as The
Wraith/Paul Sanderson/Michael Reeve

The film's visionary visual effects supervisor, Marc Kimball

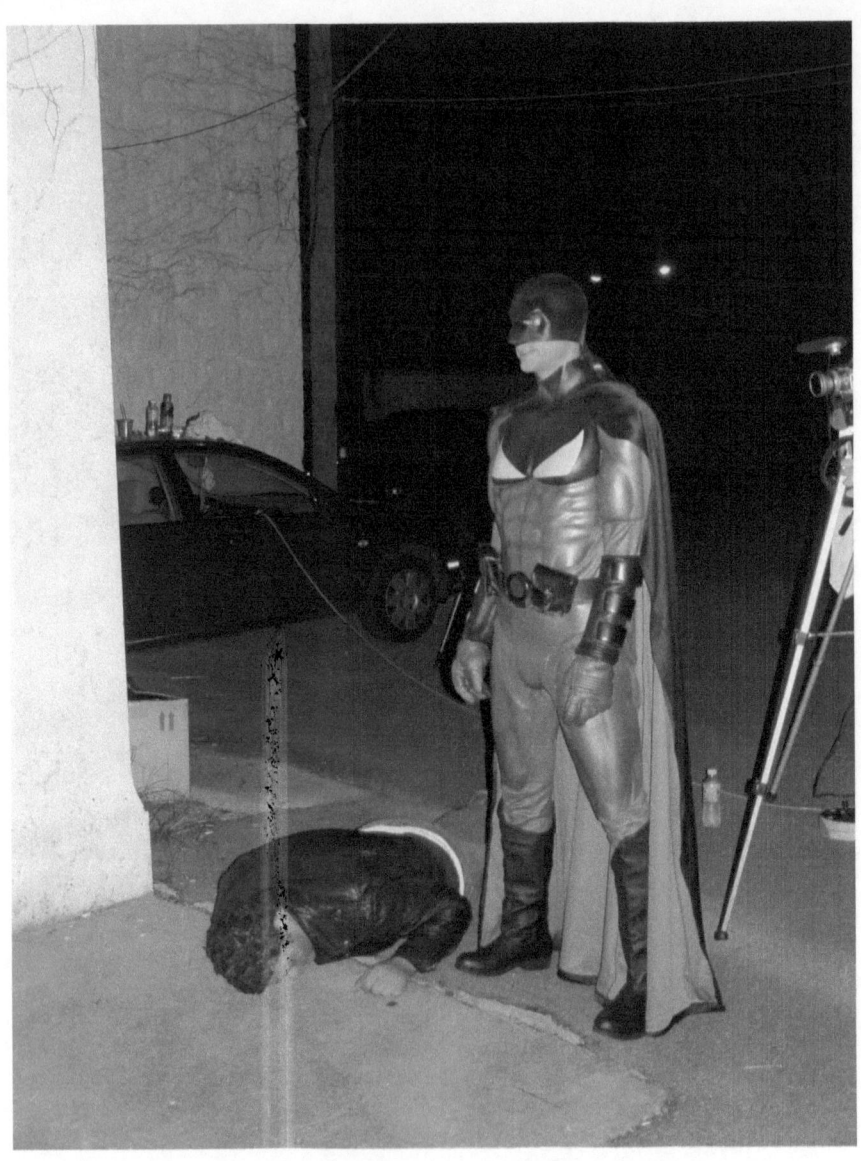

The Wraith dealing with a street thug

Stephen Semones directing a "rooftop" scene with David
Cooper as The Wraith

Leena Patterson (Stacie Cooper) and Max Horton (Nathan Blevins) confront The Wraith in The Wraith's Lair

David Cooper reading over his script

~ Also Available ~

The Wraith Adventures #2
VALLEY OF EVIL
Frank Dirscherl

After the horror the Cobra unleashed upon Metro City, Paul
Sanderson has recuperated, regained his strength and focus, and
the city has been rebuilt while its citizens have slowly started to
regroup and move forward. Into this relative calm marches Ma Tzi,
the Hong Kong drug lord, who senses a weakness in resident crime
lord Robert Latham's hold on the city and intends to exploit that
in any way necessary. And at any cost.
ISBN: 978-0-646-90809-0

AVAILABLE NOW!
www.trinitycomics.com

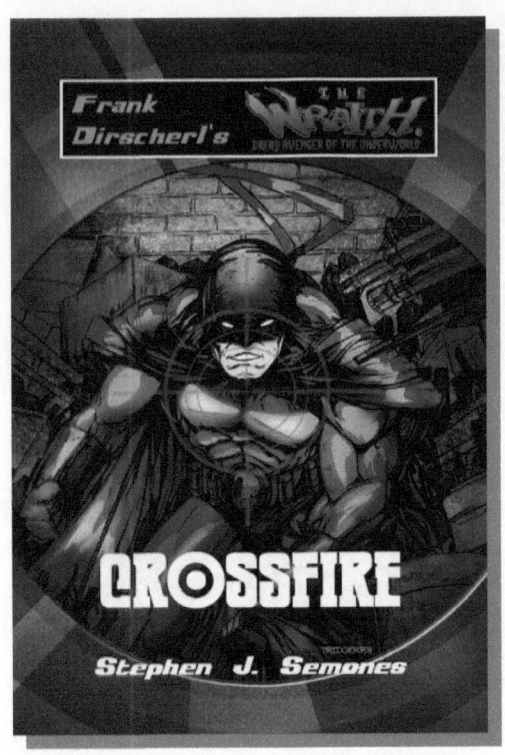

The Wraith Adventures #2.5
CROSSFIRE
Stephen J. Semones; edited by Frank Dirscherl

After a terrorist attack leaves the citizens of Metro City reeling, an
enigmatic stranger emerges from the wake of the destruction to
wage war on local crime-lord Robert Latham. In the midst of this,
Max Horton, The Wraith's right-hand man, vanishes without a
trace. Searching for Max, and for those responsible for the
devastation, The Wraith sets out for answers.

ISBN: 978-0-646-58377-8

AVAILABLE NOW!

www.trinitycomics.com

The Wraith Adventures #3
CULT OF THE DAMNED
Frank Dirscherl

With the city back firmly in his grasp, crime lord and entrepreneur
Robert Latham is celebrating by bankrolling Metro City's 200th
anniversary gala year, which includes the unveiling of a never-
before-seen ancient Aztec stone carving—the Cortes Stone—at the
City Gallery, a carving that has thrilled the scientific and artistic
communities, but infuriated the monstrous Aztekoth.
ISBN: 978-0-646-90824-3

AVAILABLE NOW!
www.trinitycomics.com

The Wraith Adventures #4
CRY OF THE WEREWOLF
Frank Dirscherl

Having gone through ordeal after ordeal, Paul Sanderson (aka The Wraith Dread Avenger of the Underworld ®) and his love Leena Patterson, decide to take a long overdue vacation. However, their idyll is soon shattered by an attack by a creature nobody thought could possibly exist—a werewolf. Soon, an evil so heinous makes himself known, and only The Wraith could possibly defeat it.
ISBN: 978-0-646-57757-9

AVAILABLE NOW!

www.trinitycomics.com

a Wraith Adventures tale

SANDERSON OF METRO
Frank Dirscherl & Bobby Nash

Two masters of the pulp fiction world, Frank Dirscherl and Bobby Nash, have come together to tell this tale, the secret NEVER before told origin of the first Wraith/Paul Sanderson, as only they could. This action-packed, atmospheric thrill could only be told now, and it could only be told by master storytellers like Dirscherl and Nash. An epic never to be repeated and not to be missed.
ISBN: 978-0-646-97923-6

AVAILABLE NOW!

www.trinitycomics.com

The Wraith short film on DVD
THE WRAITH: EYES OF JUDGMENT

This Special Edition 2-disc DVD, based on the novel *The Wraith*,
features over four hours of special features spanning two
impressive discs. With animated menus mixed in digital surround
sound, this will satisfy even the most hardcore DVD enthusiasts.
ASIN: B000F3ZTFS

AVAILABLE NOW!

www.trinitycomics.com

Join FRANK DIRSCHERL and Trinity
Comics on social media!

facebook.com/publisherTrinityComics

@Trinity_Comics

instagram.com/trinity.comics

trinitycomics.proboards.com

All Trinity Comics, The Wraith and Starflame
novels, comics and merchandise can be obtained
directly from the Trinity Comics website –
www.trinitycomics.com

Want to be The Wraith?

Well, it might be hard to actually *be* The Wraith, unless of course you, too, have been endowed with the power of the Eyes of Judgment. But you can certainly dress, drink and drive like him [*] (and you don't always have to be a millionaire to do so). See for yourselves.

The Wraith/Paul Sanderson wears:

- tailored clothing from Cad & the Dandy Tailors and Shirtmakers – www.cadandthedandy.co.uk
- bespoke footwear from Gaziano & Girling – www.gazianogirling.com
- watches from Omega (Omega Seamaster Professional black ceramic www.omegawatches.com/watch-omega-seamaster-diver-300m-co-axial-41-mm-21230412001003/
- Armani Code cologne from Giorgio Armani – www.giorgioarmanibeauty-usa.com/for-him-armani-code/for-him-armani-code,default,sc.html

drinks:

- Twinings Earl & Lady Grey tea – www.twinings.co.uk
- Keurig coffee – www.keurig.com/
- The Balvenie Scotch whisky – www.thebalvenie.com
- Armand de Brignac champagne – www.armanddebrignac.com
- Cosmopolitan cocktails

---

[*] Please note: Trinity Comics does not condone drinking and driving. **All** adults, please always drink responsibly and never drink and drive

uses:

- Dell laptops - www.dell.com.au
- Chesterfield furniture from Abbey Furniture
  www.chesterfieldfurnituremelbourne.com.au
- wallets from Launer - www.launer.com
- a Samsung Galaxy A3 cell phone -
  www.samsung.com/au/consumer/mobile-
  phone/smartphones/galaxy-a/SM-A300YZKAXSA

drives:

- a Bentley Continental GT - www.bentleymotors.com

And, if you're really eager to actually look like The Wraith—in full costume—then you can always head over to Xtreme Design FX and let Lance Coulter there make you an exact replica of the costume used for The Wraith motion picture - www.xtremedesignfx.com